DOORWAYS

a collection of short stories from members of the
Northwest Independent Writers Association

Published by the Northwest Independent Writers Association
www.niwawriters.com

ISBN: 978-1-692650-30-8

DOORWAYS

a collection of short stories from members of the
Northwest Independent Writers Association

Editor's Note

Every doorway, every intersection has a story.

—Katherine Dunn

We live in changing times. Sometimes, that change is exciting. Other times, it's terrifying. Possibilities make life interesting and, at times, paralyzing.

Doorways are a clear, tangible way to express this dichotomy. They exist *between*.

The members of NIWA, the Northwest Independent Writers Association, have taken this idea and stretched it beyond the simple, beyond the mundane, and beyond expectations.

Pick a door, any door, and find the wonder, the hope, the pain, the strange, or the absurd within.

—Lee French

Table of Contents

William Cook is a Connecticut native who moved to Oregon in 1989. He is a proud member of NIWA, and this story is his fifth appearance in the group's yearly anthology. His most recent novel, *Woman in the Waves,* is the third installment of The Driftwood Mysteries. The first of those, *Seal of Secrets,* was released this year as an audiobook. He is spending his happy retirement writing, babysitting for his fifteen grandchildren, and occasionally sneaking off to mid-week matinees at the local cineplex. Visit him at https://authorwilliamcook.com.

BAD SEED

William J. Cook

MONDAY, APRIL 22, 2019

"You were moaning in your sleep last night," my wife says over morning coffee. "Again." I hear the impatience in her voice, and I wince. She picks up the paper and reads the headlines. "It's been a couple of months. What do you suppose triggered it?"

"I don't know." I take a deep breath and let it out slowly, unable to stifle my discouragement. "The fire at Notre Dame?"

"So it's anything Catholic?"

"I guess. It's like I'm a fly in a spider's web. The more I struggle, the more tangled up I get." I don't tell her that I feel like Alice with the Red Queen, running as fast as I can to stay in the same place.

"You left fifty years ago. That's a helluva long time to be stuck. I've only known you for twenty of those years, but it's getting harder and harder for me to put up with this." Her frown darkens the room.

"But you do get some benefits, right? I make the bed every morning. I keep my side of the bathroom clean. I wash my clothes and do a good job with the dishes." My objections sound desperate, even to me.

"So you're a good soldier. I could've married somebody with obsessive-compulsive disorder and got the same thing. Your being a clean freak doesn't necessarily make me happy." The newspaper rattles her complaint as she slaps it on the table.

My shoulders slump. "I'm not the husband you signed up for, am I?" I've spent our entire marriage standing on the edge of this precipice, staring into the abyss, afraid to jump and ashamed not to.

"That's not what I said." I feel the frustration rising in her voice. It's been happening more and more over the last year. "It's just that I keep expecting you to get better. You know? Smile more. Be less irritable. Seem more content with your life. You have two beautiful grown children, and your fourth grandchild is on the way. Quit your damn poor-me routine."

She shakes her head back and forth and raises her left hand the way she does when she gets annoyed with the evening news. "Is your therapist even helping?"

She's got me on the run now, and I try to retreat. "She's a good listener. And she's smart." I pause, looking for a graceful way out. "But I don't think she really gets it."

"Gets what?" She's tapping the fingers of her right hand on the table.

"Why I left. Why I walked through that door."

"That's a good question. Why did you leave?" She glares at me, lips pursed, awaiting an answer she knows I'll avoid.

It always comes back to this. The biggest failure of my life—walking away from the seminary and the priesthood. How can I tell her why? I'm not sure I know myself. I stand and walk out of the room. "I've gotta get to work." I hear her snort of disapproval.

"Sure. You do that," she snaps at my back. "You walk away from everything when it gets hard." I grimace at the barb. Her voice catches, as though she's trying to hold back a sob. "Maybe you'll walk away from me next, like you did your first wife."

§

I drive south on 101, just as the sun crests over the Coast Range and ignites the foam of breakers crashing on the beaches to my right. My flight from God, such as it was, began and ended here, at the western limit of Oregon. It was a short, unsuccessful journey.

The clinic is a modest brick structure, one level, with offices for two psychiatrists, two nurse practitioners, one psychologist, and five clinical social workers. Coastal Behavioral Center we call ourselves. It's just north of Depoe Bay and about five miles south of my home in Driftwood. I pull into the small parking lot and enter through the STAFF ONLY door. I need to be here today.

Work usually pulls me out of my self-absorption. My problems seem so minor when I listen to those of my psychotherapy patients. They've suffered real physical trauma, afraid they were going to die—or worse. Veterans of Iraq and Afghanistan, even some old guys from Vietnam. Parents whose children were murdered in a school shooting not far from here. A woman who survived sexual abuse more horrific than anything I'd ever heard before, and I've heard a lot of stories in my thirty-five years as a clinical social worker. I am a dilettante of pain compared to them, a rank amateur, so I tread lightly and do my best to help them in their paths toward healing. They honor me by sharing their ragged lives, and I renew my vow each day never to abuse that privilege.

My last patient of the morning brings me up short. I gape at the thirty-year-old veteran of three tours in Afghanistan, the scar under his left eye, the prosthesis hidden under his pants leg.

"I think I'm going to enter the seminary. Study for the priesthood. Father O'Grady at my church thinks I have a calling. You know—a vocation."

And in an instant, I'm back there.

§

SUNDAY, OCTOBER 22, 1961

"You have a Divine Vocation, boys. God has chosen you out of the world, and you belong here." Monsignor Macallan is delivering his weekly address to us, the students of St. Francis Seminary. The school sits high on a ridge in the foothills of the Coast Range, overlooking the deep blue expanse of the Pacific Ocean. Dense Douglas firs form a barrier around the manicured lawns. The Gothic structure, with its tall tower and parapets, looks as though it would be more at home in a suburb of Paris or Vienna. I'm a freshman in high school, my first year as a seminarian at what we call "Frankie's."

We're sitting in the chapel, where the tall arches of the stained glass windows, usually kaleidoscopes of color, have gone dark after sunset, and the sweet aromas of burnt incense still linger in the air from the Benediction service earlier. The high sandstone walls radiate cold like a refrigerator, keeping us awake and alert.

The Monsignor has said the same things—and multiple variations thereof—many times before, but tonight, we all hear the edge in his voice. He's mad. Michael, a popular senior, left the seminary this morning. In a stunt we gossiped about all afternoon, he returned just before lunch, speeding up the main driveway in a bright blue convertible, his right arm around a blonde-haired young woman who laughed as we stood gawking on the sidewalk.

The veins in Macallan's head swell, and his face turns purple with rage. "Your friend Michael will burn!" he declares. "As will any of you who insult God by throwing away your vocation."

Then he changes tactics, from fear to flattery. "You have the highest calling on earth, dear boys. Each of you will become an *alter Christus*, another Christ on earth, able to forgive sins and to consecrate ordinary bread and wine into the body and blood of our Lord."

It's a heady mix indeed, stroking our egos till the underlying peril dims. Much later, we will appreciate that great power comes at great cost. In our case, it will be the sacrifice of our sexuality. Each of us will have to take a vow of celibacy, promising never to marry, never to engage in sexual intimacy with another person. We are young and foolish and think we can do that.

§

"Where did you go?"

"Forgive me. I got distracted." I feel my face redden. A therapist's nightmare—caught thinking about something else and not attending to a patient's disclosures. The very thing I promise myself not to do. Some would fire their therapist for such a faux pas, but Andrew is kind.

"That's OK. I was just saying that Father O'Grady calls it a 'delayed' vocation. He said that because of all my life experience, I would probably be more stable in the seminary than someone entering in high school or early college."

"I'm sure he's right," I manage. "We're apt to make lots more mistakes when we're young." The session concludes without further event. A quick lunch, four more patients, and a half-hour of dictation bring the day to a close. I log off my computer and head out toward the parking lot.

The sun is low in the sky, casting elongated shadows in the chill spring air. I'm driving a 13-year-old BMW that still runs like a Rolex. It's time to empty my head and my heart of the pain I've absorbed. Good loud music usually turns the trick, but not today. Andrew's story still nags at me.

I've come to believe that's what life is—stories. Stories we tell ourselves, stories that others tell us, stories we've fabricated from fragments of dreams and things we've read. The stories are never *the truth*, but rather amalgams of truth and fiction we've repeated enough times that we believe them as gospel. I'm no exception. I spend my days trying to correct the stories of others' lives while I can't amend my own.

When I pull into the garage, I see that Amy's car isn't there. I enter the kitchen and see the note on the table.

I'm going to my mother's. I think I need a break from you, and I'm sure you need a break from me. Lindsey lives just down the street, and I'll spend time with her after work. She says I'm an enabler—that I enable you to get away with all the crap you pull.

So I'm not going to do that anymore. I'm giving you time to do whatever it takes to get your act together.

My advice? Go back there. Go back to the seminary and face it once and for all. That place is your own private haunted house, filled with all the ghosts of your adolescence. Fight back, goddamn it! I swear, you've got more chains than Jacob Marley.

Anyway, just do it. When you're ready, give me a call.

I let out the breath I'd been holding while I read the letter. Knowing she's right doesn't make it any easier, but I have to do something. I can't continue living this way. I pull out my phone to check my calendar. I've got time on the books. If I get our receptionist working on it first thing tomorrow, I'll have her move up all my patients into extra hours between Tuesday and Thursday, freeing me to go to Frankie's on Friday.

I shake my head back and forth. It's a pilgrimage I've avoided for fifty years—the way I go around streets that I know have a Catholic Church on them, skip movies with any reference to priests. The only exception has been my attention to the nightly news on television. How often have I sat like an unquiet acolyte before the TV, terrified I would recognize the name of a former classmate as the latest perpetrator of sexual abuse by a priest? I walk to the liquor cabinet and pour myself three fingers of Irish whiskey.

That night the demons come back. I've never told Amy that I hear voices sometimes, reminding me of all the things I've done wrong in my life. Once I even saw Macallan, sitting at the foot of my bed like Banquo's ghost. Occasionally, I've felt his presence in my bedroom, as I'm drifting off to sleep. Then I jump as though I've just touched an electric outlet. I know. I've got all the classic symptoms. So why don't I take medication? I usually tell myself that I don't want the sedation and the side effects. But when I'm alone like this, I wonder if a part of me thinks I deserve what I get.

As Amy said, I'm a good soldier. While the days are flying by, I keep the kitchen clean, make the bed, sort the mail into *his* and *hers* stacks. I even vacuum the rug in the living room. Amy's forever teasing me about it, saying I act as if the Pope were about to pay us a surprise visit. I laugh it off, never explaining that it's a tool I use to keep my anxiety in check.

When Friday finally comes, I'm not ready. My stomach is tied in knots, and it's all I can do to get a cup of coffee down. But no excuses. It's now or never. After my shower, I put on a white shirt and tie, dark pants, and a sports coat—the traditional daily dress at Frankie's. I take a last look around the house, as though afraid I might not come back, but really just stalling for time. My grandiose fantasy suggests I'm the Knight Errant embarking on a quest to slay the dragon, but I'm sure the reality will be far more ordinary than that.

I drive south to Newport under a canopy of gray cloud. The weather report said the rain will be here by noon, but I'll bet that was an overly optimistic prediction. Sure enough, I haven't gone two miles before a fine mist mottles the windshield. In a moment, a light but steady rain is playing a familiar rhythm on the roof of my car—classic Northwest percussion. I turn left at the old road and begin to climb into the hills.

How different it all looks. Eager buyers, fleeing the bloated highways of California, are staking claims to the forest. Frankie's is no longer tucked away from the world behind a wall of Douglas firs. Neighborhoods encroach upon its spacious lawns.

I stop at the base of the main driveway and look up to the crest. Silhouetted against the weeping sky are the stark battlements of the seminary, looking like an ancient castle, complete with its foreboding tower. A thrill of panic makes my body shiver. It's been so long since I've seen this massive edifice, this place of power. The panorama takes my breath away.

Four other cars are parked around the front circle. I pull in behind a black SUV. Before entering the main building, I decide to walk around the campus, check all the old hangouts. Thankful I've brought a trench coat and a hat, I brave the rain and stalk around the senior dormitories. The enormous ginkgo tree, with its fan-shaped leaves, still presides over this corner. Every fall it would burst into its brilliant yellow finery, an explosion of autumn sun against an azure sky. Today, the stately gentleman's cloak is an olive green. A keeper of secrets, it's been a witness to all that transpired during Frankie's reign on this hill. I lay my hand on its trunk, sure it recognizes me, wondering what stories it would tell if it could.

A few more paces bring me to a widening of the path on the way to the tennis courts and beyond—the Butt Grounds, the only place on campus where seminarians could smoke, and most did. Cigarettes were a part of our daily ritual, something to do during breaks between study halls, after meals, before night prayers. Rain or shine, sleet or snow, we were out there, backs to the wind, huddled together, bound by clouds of tobacco smoke. I had quit cigarettes reluctantly at the age of twenty-five, ten years after I had begun smoking. I still miss them.

Another fifty yards, and I'm surprised that no one's been minding the tennis courts. Several trees, now almost twenty feet tall, have sprouted up in the middle of them, making me feel as though I'm walking through the set of a post-apocalyptic movie—civilization wiped out, the earth reabsorbing the detritus of society. That feeling is heightened when I reach the handball courts, now enshrouded with English ivy, completely obscuring the sixteen-foot walls in tangles of green vines.

Wading through the knee-deep plants on the surface of the courts, my last bit of exploring takes me to the pond. As I push my way past shrubs that had once been a path, I feel cold rain sneak past my collar and trickle down the back of my neck. When I look ahead, I find there is no pond. The dam must have been taken out decades ago, draining our playground. I'm surrounded by a young, almost impenetrable forest where once we had poled our trusty raft, hunting for painted turtles and fishing for bullheads.

A kind of melancholy settles over me, as gently as the rain. What had I expected? I hear the poet whisper, *"Things fall apart; the centre cannot hold;/ Mere anarchy is loosed upon the world,/"*[1]

I force my way back through the jungle. I have an appointment to keep.

Ten minutes later, as I approach the intimidating structure, I see the cornerstone to the right of the front doors. Its inscription brings me to a halt.

SPES MESSIS IN SEMINE

1928

The translation of the Latin rolls off my tongue. *The Hope of the Harvest is in the Seed.*

But what about the seed that doesn't sprout? The bad seed?

When I walk through the front door, I recall that, as a seminarian, I had used this door only once a year, when registering in September. Inside is much the same as it had been—marble floors, three broad steps leading up to the doors of the chapel and to the main hallway. To the immediate right is the office. A gray-haired receptionist now sits where the Sacristan had once done secretarial tasks between episodes of homework and duties in the sanctuary. She looks over a computer screen and greets me.

"May I help you?"

I fumble for words. "I used to go to school here." I'm not sure what kind of expression is on my face, or if it matters to her. "A long time ago. Is it OK if I look around? I don't mean to disturb anybody."

---

1. "The Second Coming," by William Butler Yeats, 1919.

She smiles. "We get that all the time. You're one of what we call 'the Old Guard.' I don't see a Roman collar. Your day off?"

"No," I confess. "Never made it all the way to the priesthood." I feel my face get warm.

"Most didn't. Feel free to explore. You do know we're not St. Francis Seminary anymore, don't you? Now we're just administrative offices for the Archdiocese, though we do have some conference rooms for meetings. And we use the chapel for parish retreats."

"That explains why the grounds out back have fallen into…" Again, I search for the right words. "…some disrepair."

Her smile broadens. "The tennis and handball courts? We can't seem to get the funds to restore them since nobody lives here anymore. I'm sure you can understand."

"Yeah. Money's tight everywhere. Well, thank you. I'll just wander a bit. I won't be long."

She nods and returns to her computer.

I leave the office and climb the steps. The large oak doors of the chapel beckon me. My heart skips a beat. "Not yet," I tell myself as I back away.

The hallway I'm in is hung with old paintings of saints and photographs of former rectors and bishops, unchanged from days of yore, except for one addition. I see Macallan's picture hanging there, bald head gleaming, crimson sash—what we called his "red belly band"—around his opulent waist. If I didn't know better, I'd describe his smile as "angelic."

To the right, the hall leads to what had been the refectory, our dining room. I walk toward it, listening carefully. I can almost hear the sounds of cutlery on dinner plates and the buzz of conversations. Amy always had trouble believing the stories I told her about the food—the morning I found a centipede in our oatmeal, the evening of the ants in the egg noodles. We ate bad food with equally bad names—monkey dicks, mystery loaf, kangaroo meat, hockey pucks. I stayed thin until I left.

I turn and walk back in the other direction, toward what we called "Hogan's Alley," the priests' private quarters. I would meet my confessor there for weekly Penance and spiritual direction, in a dark-paneled room that smelled of leather and tobacco. Preparation for that encounter would be a thorough examination of conscience. Had I spoken angrily to a fellow seminarian? Had I taken the Lord's name in vain? More importantly, had I consented to impure thoughts? We never used the term "masturbation." It was "self abuse," a big ticket item. It was called a "mortal sin," a category it shared with murder and adultery. Those who die with that sort of sin on their souls go straight to Hell for all eternity.

Before I realize I've turned back around, I'm standing before the immense doors of the chapel. I lay my hands on the polished oak and imagine them thrumming with the energy that dwells within. I feel like Bilbo at the threshold of Smaug's den. As I grasp one of the handles and pull the heavy door open, I can hear the priest beginning the Mass with his Latin incantation:

Introibo ad altare Dei.
Ad Deum qui laetificat iuventutem meam.

I will go in to the altar of God.
To God who gives joy to my youth.

I enter the dim enclosure, lit only by the stained glass windows with their vivid reds and blues and yellows. In the twilight ahead, hanging above the altar, is the red sanctuary lamp, its flickering candle standing vigil over the consecrated bread—the Body of Christ—present in the golden tabernacle. Suspended on the back wall is an enormous sculpture of the crucified Jesus.

I can't catch my breath. Sweat bathes my face. My hands are shaking, and my knees wobble. I stumble forward and grasp the back of one of the pews to keep myself from falling.

"Panic attack," my clinician self tells me. "You won't faint. That takes low blood pressure. Yours has spiked. Distract yourself from your physical symptoms. Any mindless exercise will do."

I begin to count the rows of pews. When I've done that forward and backward, I start numbering the candles in the sanctuary. Then I'm picking out individual panes in the nearest stained glass window. After a few minutes, my breathing returns to normal, and I sit down.

This is the heart of my haunting. This is where I had spent my adolescence, aching with loneliness, ashamed that I didn't feel holy, angry that I couldn't stop imagining what it would feel like to have a girlfriend. The hours on my knees, the drudgery of prayer and meditation, the fear of sexual temptation. When I had decided at last that I could not take the vow of celibacy, I had tried to escape, but failed.

I remember that little boy of fourteen, sitting on this stiff wooden bench decades ago, flush with ambition and idealism. He had imagined himself a gallant warrior fighting in the battle of good versus evil, embarking on a quest to save souls. Lulled by seductive words and traditions, by the adulation of his parents, he had never seen what lurks here in the shadows.

That adolescent is the Tar-Baby from whom I can't get unstuck. Of all the stories I've told myself, this is the most egregious. All my life, I've been the judge-penitent, accusing myself of betrayal, condemning myself to fevered dreams and half-truths. Looking up at the vaulted ceiling high overhead, the walls of hard stone, the cold glass, I finally understand what that frightened boy could not.

No loving Father dwells here. This is not the home of his son Jesus, who told his disciples to let the little children come to him. It's Zeus in disguise, fulminating from Mount Olympus, demanding sacrifice. Or better, Saturn eating his children. That thought staggers me. Who knows what perversions a god like that could lead his minions to perform?

I sit there and bury my face in my hands. I weep. I shed tears for myself and for all the young boys who had been sacrificed on that altar. What scares me most is what I might have become had I remained. What if I had taken the vow of celibacy, condemning myself to a life of infantile relationships, without normal adult intimacy? I tremble as I recall again the horrendous reports of sexual abuse committed by priests—hundreds and hundreds, all over the globe, a litany of unspeakable crimes. Would I have become one of those unholy malefactors? Would I have fallen into that awful gravity, victimizing children who were as innocent as I had once been? The revelation blinds me. *Who knows what perversions he could lead his minions to perform?*

I am not a Knight Errant after all, only a wayfarer, one pilgrim among many. I had imagined my sword would be my upraised arm, fist clenched in defiance; my shield, my ability to reason and my years of training as a therapist. But it's not like that at all.

Instead, it's a kind of disappointment. The dragon cannot be slain, only kept at bay. A deep weariness washes over my body and soul, like a receding tide sweeping debris from the beach. I feel exhausted but cleansed, more at peace with myself than I have been in years. I take a deep breath and exhale slowly, allowing that new-found calm to penetrate to my core. I'm not a failure, not a bad seed, despite the story I've been telling myself since I left St. Francis. My instincts had been accurate from the beginning. There is no shame in what I had done, however incomplete. I can finish my escape today.

"No!" I shout aloud, the word echoing in the cavern of the Beast, mingling with the cries of all those forgotten children, wailing in the dark. "No," I repeat with firm conviction. "You couldn't have me then, and you can't have me now."

I stand as straight and tall as I can manage, turn, and walk toward the exit. I go through that doorway one final time, whole and free, ransomed at last.

Outside, the rain has stopped. The air has been washed clean, perfumed by something blooming nearby. It feels good on my face and tastes sweet when I breathe. I pull the phone from my pocket to make the call.

Amy answers on the first ring.

Emma Lee is a native Californian wanderer enthralled by the copious amounts of rain in the Pacific Northwest. She enjoys gardening and the challenges of parenting two neurodiverse teenagers. Family is front and center in her women's fiction and contemporary romance stories.

THE FRONT DOOR

Emma Lee

The cavernous home improvement store had swallowed me, cutting me off from time and space. For some reason, the bare concrete floors, impossibly high ceilings, and faint smell of sawdust pushed aside all other thoughts so I could focus on my goal.

Before me, doors hung in rows, each with tiny variations. Glass cutouts in different shapes and sizes seemed popular. Conventional square patterns dominated the racks. Plain, flat doors huddled at one end to avoid contaminating the good stuff with their cheapness.

"Can I help you?"

I glanced at the young gentleman in the bright blue shop apron who spoke to me. His nametag read *Tyler*. The me of twenty years ago would've flirted with his rugged, muscular self. On this day, I didn't want to deal with a man.

If I wanted to complete my quest, though, Tyler could undoubtedly help me. He had that aura of a guy who knows his way around a power saw.

"I want to replace my front door, but I'm not really sure what I'm looking for." I also needed to replace the garage door, but my bank account couldn't handle both at once.

Tyler smiled without showing his teeth and nodded. "Is your existing one damaged?"

"No." I smirked. "My ex-husband likes it."

"Oh." My answer had surprised him but not in the fun, happy way. He struggled with his expression, finally settling on polite interest. "Do you know what you're not looking for?"

I've always appreciated people who know how to ask good questions. Tyler had won my trust, at least on the subject of doors. "Green. I'm looking for not green."

He gestured to the doors, none of which featured green. "That doesn't narrow it down much. How about solid wood versus metal?"

How much did I know about front doors? Very little. I shrugged.

"My neighborhood is safe, in the suburbs. It's full of cookie-cutter houses, soccer moms, and over-the-top Halloween displays. I think I'd rather have one with glass. Beyond that, I have no idea."

"Most people have no idea," Tyler said with a friendly nod. Did he patronize me? A little, maybe?

At least he didn't give me the same macho "I'll take care of that for you, little lady" vibe I got at the oil change place.

"Let me walk you through what we've got and explain the differences." He picked a door with a small glass pane in the center and embarked upon a verbal and visual tour of my options.

Replacing the front door represented the most budget-feasible way of removing one of the last, lingering smears of Jack's influence from my life. I couldn't afford to move to a new house. Even if I could magically find something within my budget after replacing most of the furniture and repainting several walls, I didn't want to force my two teenagers to change schools.

As Tyler reached the point of trying to explain subtle differences, I held up a hand to get him to stop. That stuff would fly over my head at the speed of light. Jack would've listened intently, understood none of it, and pretended like he knew more.

"Which ones would you use for your own home?" I asked.

Tyler grinned and pointed out two. "Those are my top choices."

One had a small, inoffensive oval-shaped cutout with beveled, frosted glass. The other had a larger square pane with dividers, alternating types of occluded glass, and strips of frosted glass. More, fancier glass resulted in a higher cost, so I took a good, long look at the oval one.

Jack would hate it. That sold the door to me. Besides, it looked fine.

"I'll take this one. Do you install them? I'm sure I would mess it up if I tried, and I have no idea how to dispose of the old one." Not to mention I didn't have time for any of that.

Between my job and shuttling my kids, I barely had time to breathe some days. Jack didn't live close enough to have regular visitations. He'd moved in with Becky, and she lived two hours from our house. They only had a one-bedroom apartment anyway.

For his visitation, Jack showed up on the first Saturday of the month and took the kids for the day. Nothing more. He hadn't wanted more.

The kids hated it. I hated it. Jack acted like he did us the world's greatest favor by showing up and doing his damned job as a father for ten hours a month.

"I can find someone to do that, yes," Tyler said, snapping me out of my thoughts. "Let's go write this up." He escorted me to his workstation and tapped on a computer. I gave him my name and address, and opened my purse to find my credit card.

"Are you looking to replace the locks too?"

I hadn't even considered doing so. Jack had given up his keys. Nothing had prevented him from making copies, of course. Why would he want to sneak into the house, though, when he had Becky?

Then again, I didn't know Becky well. She might have a vindictive streak. If she'd gotten hold of his keys and made a copy, she might do something. Even with the length of the drive, I couldn't discount the possibility.

I sighed. "Yes. That's a good idea. I should probably have the lock changed on the back door too. I might as well get brand new doorknobs for both while I'm at it. They're kind of grungy."

"Do you want to replace the back door too? A contractor will charge for the visit, plus hourly, so if you think you might want to, you might as well do both at once."

When we bought the house, the realtor had lost the front door key. Not as in lost forever, or we would've demanded she do something about it. She'd put it in the wrong place. The back door key, though, she'd still had on hand when we took possession. Good enough for us.

Jack had swooped me off my feet and carried me over the threshold of the back door to our first house. I remembered the smell of his aftershave. I also remembered the door smacking into the wall because he shoved it open too hard.

We never did properly repair the dent left by the knob.

That memory twisted my stomach into knots. I wanted to step back in time and shake some sense into that woman. How long had it taken the shine to wear off? Five years, give or take.

Twelve years of business trips and excuses. Only after he'd slipped enough for me to learn about Becky with no effort had I taken off the blinders. By then, I think he'd almost wanted me to discover his chronic infidelity. He'd seemed relieved when I'd confronted him.

Becky probably wouldn't last more than a year.

"Carrie?" Tyler asked.

I'd fallen into woolgathering, apparently. "Yes, let's replace the back door. Just something plain and white is fine. Whatever's appropriate for that. No window. You seem to know what you're talking about, so I trust your judgment."

"Are you okay?"

I frowned at the counter, not truly seeing the helpful notice suggesting

I ask about a quote for water heater servicing. "It's only been final for a week, and it was fast. He moved out to live with Becky three months ago."

Lucky me, my lawyer had squeezed Jack dry despite Washington state's community property laws, so I had almost everything. Until we'd gone over the numbers, I hadn't realized how much debt we'd carried. Business trips, my ass. I deserved all this mess for letting him handle the bills and never worrying about any of it, I supposed.

We ate enough, the bills got paid, and I could afford to put gas in my car. What more had I needed?

"Oh." His brow scrunched. "I'm…sorry? I guess?" Shaking off his indecision, he patted my hand. The gesture comforted me in some small measure. He made me feel like I mattered. "Are you sure you want to do this now? I can put it in as a quote instead of an order, and you can think about it."

Holding up my credit card, I shook my head. "No, I need to do this. Thank you, though. It's nice of you to ask."

Tyler took my card to pay for my new doors and locks. "You must be the one who everybody relies on to be strong."

"Sorry?"

He smiled as he tapped keys on his computerized register. "Every family has that one person who doesn't buckle under the stress and supports everyone else."

"Until they do buckle," I murmured. My father had been like that. Two weeks after his diagnosis, he'd died in a car accident. No one could prove he'd driven the car into that bridge support on purpose, but we all knew. His final act had shouted a giant middle finger at his life insurance company because they couldn't deny Mom the payout despite his apparent suicide.

His auto insurance policy had paid out too. Take that, jerks.

Glancing at me as he swiped my card, Tyler frowned. "Would you like to get coffee?"

I blinked at him. "Coffee?"

"Hot water run through crushed beans? A bit bitter, some people add cream and sugar? Available next door?" He handed back my card.

"Oh. Right." For a moment, I thought he'd asked me on a date. In no way did I meet any of the criteria for Tyler. He needed some fresh young thing without a lot of baggage to cart around. But no, he probably wanted to make sure I didn't leave and kill myself. Decent people did things like that. As far as I could tell, Tyler was a decent person.

Him asking me out for coffee still seemed weird, but spending fifteen minutes with a decent person in a public place didn't sound like a bad idea.

"Sure. I've got some time." My teenagers had to suffer with their father all day anyway.

We finished the paperwork. The contractor could take up to two weeks to contact me. After I signed everything, Tyler escorted me out of the store and to the coffee shop.

He opened the door for me with a cheerful smile.

Once upon a time, Jack had opened doors for me. Thinking back, I supposed he'd stopped doing that around the time he'd started cheating on me. Why bother offering polite gestures to his wife when he had a girlfriend to fawn over?

I should've noticed. How did I not see it? What could I have done to keep him from straying?

I'd never looked at another man with more than passing, fleeting interest. Even standing in line with Tyler, I didn't know how to see him as anything other than a piece of performance art to admire in his surroundings.

"I'll buy," Tyler said. "What do you want?"

"You don't have to do that."

He leaned close. "No, I don't, but I'm offering anyway. What would you like?"

Something about his voice or the scent of his sweat and faint cologne with a sawdust kicker made me blush. "Mocha latte," I mumbled like a ditzy schoolgirl given attention by her older crush.

He ordered for me and paid for it with cash. Jack had never once ordered for me. I couldn't decide how I felt about it. Tyler had asked what I wanted, then handled the transaction. Having to put in my own order on my rare excursions with Jack hadn't made me feel put-upon or unloved. Tyler asking and taking control didn't make me feel like I'd missed something.

We sat at a small table to wait for our drinks. I didn't know what to say, and couldn't look at him. The moment made me shift, too awkward about the situation to sit still.

"Are you getting enough sleep since he left?"

"Sleep? Yes, I think so." He sounded like my kids' therapist all of a sudden.

My daughter had asked for therapy immediately. I'd made her younger brother go too. I didn't have time for regular sessions, but accompanied the kids when they requested it.

"It's not like everything was sunshine and roses and then he up and left. We've been drifting apart for a long time. This wasn't shocking."

Watch me lie like a pro. The shock still rippled through me as I lay in bed every night, staring at the bedroom door like I thought he would return home early from his latest trip. As if he'd ever come home early.

Before The Discussion, I'd never watched the door like that. After it, I couldn't stop.

"I don't even know what I miss."

The barista called Tyler's name.

He stood to get our drinks. "Your comfortable routine." With that, he left me to ponder his statement.

Routine, I got. Yes, I had to admit I didn't like all the upheaval. The kids didn't either.

Comfortable? Not so much.

Tyler set a steaming cup in front of me and sat. "The comfort of knowing what to expect is what I mean. Maybe everything wasn't great, but it was your normal. You got used to it, like you get used to the quirks of your boss or coworkers. He doesn't pick up his socks, so you pick them up and get annoyed about it. Again and again. After a while, it's comfortable even if you hate it."

I furrowed my brow. "Do you moonlight as a therapist?"

He laughed. "No. My parents divorced when I was twelve, and I had some trouble adjusting in college. I've seen my fair share of shrinks."

"My kids are fourteen and fifteen." I popped the lid off my coffee and blew on it.

He gently bumped my shoulder. "You don't look old enough to have teenagers."

"You don't look old enough to flirt with me," I shot back.

With the air of someone trying hard not to make a mistake, he directed his attention to his coffee. "Then I'll have to just ask you out. Would you like to have dinner with me tonight?"

What? "Dinner? Like a date? With me?"

"Wow." Tyler covered my hand with his and met my gaze with inscrutable, uncomfortable intensity. "You're an attractive woman. I promise he didn't cheat on you because of your looks."

I blushed so hard my cheeks hurt. "Thank you."

"I don't know you very well, but I seriously doubt it had anything at all to do with you." Picking up my hand and turning it over to reveal my palm, he rubbed his rough, callused thumbs over my skin.

A shiver wriggled over my body and couldn't remember how to interpret it.

"I admire your strength and determination," he said, smiling at me like he thought I had value. "I also appreciate the ability to make a snap decision about something that matters yet doesn't, like a front door."

This young man I'd met maybe an hour earlier kissed my palm. All kinds of things inside me flared with a fire I hadn't experienced in a long time. My imagination clanked into life, struggling past all the years of disuse, to try to picture him without his shirt.

Tyler definitely had abs.

"Have dinner with me," he said.

"I, um." My mouth refused to work properly. "I'm not really sure…"

He shifted closer and smiled like he knew what I looked like naked. "I'm fine with being your distracting rebound fling." Whatever he saw on my face made him chuckle. "Or just having dinner. No pressure." He let go of my hand and wrote on a scrap of paper from his apron pocket.

What was happening?

"This is my phone number," he said as he placed the paper in my hand. "Call me whenever you're ready to."

While I fumbled for some kind of response, he stood, snatched up his coffee cup, and left.

The door shut behind him. I stared at it, seeing nothing.

When I'd decided to replace my front door, I hadn't imagined a bizarre adventure like this.

I looked at the paper in my hand and tried to make sense of it. Tyler had given me his phone number in neat, printed letters and numbers. He wanted to see me again. Our coffee excursion hadn't turned him off, it had added to his interest.

He knew I had teenagers and a recent divorce, and he still wanted to date me. Maybe he thought I had a lot of money and could provide for him so he could quit his job. Except he'd insisted upon paying for my coffee. He'd suggested a fling, not a long-term relationship.

In a daze, I picked up my cup and stumbled to my minivan. Somehow, I got home without causing an accident. I parked the car in the driveway out of habit because the garage door didn't work. Jack had backed his car into it from the outside and dented it far enough out of shape to wedge it in place.

We'd never scraped together the money to fix it. He'd spent numerous weekends in Portland, Seattle, and Vancouver staying at fancy hotels with other women, and I'd lived without a functional garage door.

Or, for that matter, a functional husband.

For the first time, I wanted to destroy something. Rage swelled in my chest. All this time, I'd bobbled along, treading water. Suddenly, everything crashed over me in a furious wave. I had to restrain myself to avoid getting back into the car to ram it through the garage door or the front wall of the house.

The ugly eyesore of a front door in its dull dark green hung like an oozing gob of pus. To get inside, I had to touch it when I wanted to throw a chair through the window.

I'd put up with so many things. I'd shopped at thrift stores, bought the cheap cuts of meat, and clipped coupons because we didn't have any money. Our kids had never had more than a handful of toys each. We didn't even have cable or internet service at the house. He'd found space in the budget for my cheap, crappy cellphone so I could get notices from the kids' schools.

All this time, he'd wined and dined a neverending conga line of younger women. We'd suffered so he could impress mistress after mistress at our expense.

Standing in the front yard and glaring at the hideous door, I screamed my rage. Obscenities flew from my mouth, directed at the door as if Jack stood in front of it. If he'd shown up at that moment, I would've killed him with my bare hands.

After a few minutes, my energy wore down. The anger remained, simmering in a cauldron inside me. I sagged and covered my face.

Jack still got to prance around with Becky and shirk his responsibilities while I didn't. I'd never pranced. Even before I met Jack, I hadn't cut loose and indulged in wild parties or casual hookups.

I stuck my hand in my pocket and fetched Tyler's phone number. The crumpled paper felt like a lifeline.

As I unlocked the door and stepped inside, I pulled out my phone and texted him to accept his dinner date.

Time for me to prance.

Sheri J. Kennedy is a visual artist as well as an author. Thoughtful curiosity influences all her pursuits. She studied philosophy, literature and communications for a B.A. in Humanities. As owner of FVP Books/FreeValley Publishing, she supports independent authors. Sheri grapples with grief, but joy is her middle name. Life is rich with her husband in a little house by the river in the mountains near Seattle. Novels: *Feeling Human* and *Likeness*. She's also published as Kennedy J. Quinn.

HALLWAY LIGHT

Sheri J. Kennedy

When I was a child my mother left my bedroom door open a crack and the light on in the hallway. After many a nightmare, I clung to that bright crack as a beacon to another world. A safe place only a leap away. I longed for such a beacon this spring when I was orphaned. Orphaned at forty-four may seem like nothing, but somehow it snuffed out that comforting light in the hallway.

Grief descended like hoarfrost on the buds that strove to bring color to my gardens this year. And by the time I thawed from my murky freeze, clinging blackberry vines choked my backyard cutting off all passage to the river beyond. Today by sheer grit, I tackled them. Trying to gain some measure of control over life gone wild. While tussling with an aggressive gnarly creeper, the clippers dropped, and blood dripped from yet another thorn's piercing. I leaned into the rough embrace of an old fir tree. The nearby rushing river called. Urging me to break through the impregnable barbed barrier and float away. The flagrant light of summer exposed my misery, and even the soaring evergreens couldn't provide enough shade to ease it.

A deep breath of air failed to refresh me. Redolent of over-ripe blackberries, it lay heavy with fruitless hope of escape. Heat-burdened sunrays slanted in, scorching all beneath the overhanging maples. Patches of shade lengthened to stark shadows. I craved the hidden depths of their inky black shelter. The burning orb, suspended over treetops on the opposing bank, scrutinized me without mercy. Its unforgiving glare tortured all effort. Fortitude failed. Perhaps I'd try for the river another day.

I wrestled the unwieldy waste bag attempting to hold the tenacious vines I'd gathered. Bent at the base of a towering cedar, chasing briars that defied containment, I stopped dead in my tracks. A tall crack of cool shadow ran up the trunk of the cedar – the meeting of two mighty roots. The slice of deep black enthralled my grief-ridden spirit like the slice of bright light had held me as a child.

HALLWAY LIGHT

With a glance at the river, I recoiled from the blazing sun, and reached for the darkness. My world-weary touch parted the heavy hoary roots of the cedar. The lightless crevasse that gaped at my feet beckoned to me like the doorway to my childhood hallway. I leaped to the internal night like I'd leaped from my nightmare-ridden bed to the safety of the light beyond.

Instead of a reassuring thud of terrazzo floor, black silence enveloped me.

§

When the woman parted the shaggy-shod foot of the colossal cedar, she tore into my lightless limbo, exposing me wide to the piercing bright day. In luminescent terror, the deepness of my shadow spread thin, but triumphed as she leaped to my retracting blackness. Caught in my numbing arms. Enveloped in torpid nothingness. I felt her longing for silent forgetfulness. Her surrender to the peace that descends when inky night eternal, snuffs out the senses of the soul. Her weary form floated, suspended in my sea of darkness. And my murky fingers wound her ethereal gloom into a silent shroud destined for obscurity in the depths of midnight's umbra.

But in the final squeeze of her spirit's twilight into night, a crack of light pierced my shady purpose dispelling gloom in a narrow beam of fierce hope. The radiant memory sliced the shroud, and gathering blackness parted releasing blazing beauty, in her soul embedded, back into the day from whence it came. She gasped from her bed of enlightened moss as my dense darkness snapped back with a crack into the cedar's enduring foundation. Retreating from the evening sun that lit her face with life.

Heidi Hansen learned the power of words at a young age. Two books of her short stories have been published, *A Slice of Life* and *A Second Slice*. Heidi co-founded Olympic Peninsula Authors and has edited two volumes of *In The Words Of Olympic Peninsula Authors*. She is also as a member of Northwest Independent Writers Association. In Sequim, WA., Heidi leads a spontaneous writing group at the library and hosts a monthly open mic for writers.

In the July/August 2019 issue of Writer's Digest she was the short story winner for "The Last Time I Saw Billy."

GAMBIT

Heidi Hansen

Each year I dreamt of dressing in costume for the Gamers' Convention, aka "The Con." But my fear of not fitting in or being laughed at, nixed that desire. Listening to my friends reminisce about a game they participated in the year before, convinced me that I should get more involved this year. After all, if I was playing along with others, I would fit in. This year the Con was held at a multi-story convention center; taking over all the halls and ballrooms.

"Go to the game room and sign up to play. You'll be dealt a player card, and given instructions," Paul added.

"The rules of the game are organic," my friend Karen warned.

"The costumes are amazing, and it'll blow your mind," Suzann added.

Based on their recommendation, I headed straight to the game room at the Con.

A red-bearded young man hastily whispered the rules of the game in the darkened hallway after he dealt me a card. Unlike a playing card, it was an eight by eleven sheet of pale green card stock with orange letters printed on one side. "Show your card when you suspect another player in proximity. Find the players for the game to begin."

"What?" I said stepping back. "How do I…" Asking was a waste of time as he turned and vanished.

A brunette cheerleader stepped in front of me. The teenaged girl carried a similar-sized white card tucked under her arm as if it mandated authority. I wondered if she was a part of the game. I touched the "Liberty For All" card I had been dealt, keeping the message concealed, snug against my body.

Not sure about my next step, I decided to follow the cheerleader. She was moving fast, and I had to double-time to catch up. She turned the corner and floated down a stairway. I was on her tail. A figure of speech. She did not have an actual tail as far as I could see, but other Con-goers we passed did have tails and ears, some had horns, more than two in one case.

All the costumed attendees stood out from those dressed in street clothes. Head down, I melted into the crowd in my usual jeans and t-shirt.

"Wait," I wanted to call out, but I needed to verify that she was in the game. Maybe she'd lead me to other players, maybe to the game.

After three flights, she stepped into a hallway and stopped at a door. She opened it after a quick rap, then flashed the card to someone inside and exited. I positioned myself to see her card. "Five Minutes" it read. She repeated this process down the hallway, eleven times in all. No one joined up.

She stopped, turned and faced me in the empty hallway. I almost collided with her.

"Are you following me?" she demanded in a husky growl.

"Yes," I admitted.

"Do I know you?" Her brown eyes bore into mine.

"Er," I stuttered and pulled out my card, revealing it to her.

"Oh," she said. "You're one of them."

I stepped back. *Wasn't she one of us? Had I erred in proclaiming my play?*

"Wait here," she said touching my arm gently, and darted around the corner.

I waited five minutes. Just like her card said, if that mattered. Behind me, the doors opened. People poured out of the rooms, surrounding me as they made their way through the hallway. I circled, watching them for signs. I feared the cheerleader wasn't coming back. *Would she send other players to me? Really, why did I want to get into this stupid game in the first place?*

Then I realized the connection between her sign and the people spilling into the halls. She was a timekeeper, not a player. My spirits fell, I was not fitting in. I began to shuffle my way back to the main hall of the Con.

A door slammed. Hearing heavy footfalls behind me, I turned to see a seven-foot giant advancing toward me. At my full height, I barely reached his chest. He was dressed in animal skins and looked like a Neanderthal. The skins were real because as he neared, the skins stunk of decay and sweat.

"Ew!" I cried. My eyes burned from the stench. He reached inside his furry shroud and flashed a card, "Missing Link."

"Oh," I said, and showed him my card.

There was a twinkle of surprise in his eyes, then he bowed formally from the waist.

Now what?

He motioned for me to follow and turned back the way he had come.

I smirked. He lumbered as you might suspect an actual Neanderthal would. I thought he played his part to the hilt. *What should I be doing in my role? Where would I get a costume?* I followed, keeping a respectable distance so that I could breathe.

I followed him back down the corridor, around the corner and into the stairwell. Down one floor, then another. Wooden planks replaced the cement steps, creaking under the weight of the Neanderthal.

Another floor down, the fluorescent lights switched to torch-like sconces, unless they were actual torches. Black smoke smudged the walls above them showing me they were real.

I questioned why I was following this ape-like giant. Was it only because he had a card? Was he the missing link for me to join the game? *Should I turn back?*

Voltar or Sasquatch, whoever he was, thudded through a doorway and into a dark corridor. I followed. He didn't check to see if I was still behind him. He trudged ahead. The torch lights flickered as he passed. Then the lights went out.

"Oy," I cried. Another door slammed. It was metal and heavy; there was a definite clank when it shut behind me. I shuddered.

"Hello?" I called out. "Anyone?" I felt my heart thumping. For a moment, I heard other sounds, human or animal; I was uncertain. I wasn't sure if they were cries of anger, fear, or triumph. Those sounds swirled around me in the darkness. A cold shiver ran down my spine. Fear gripped me. *What had I gotten myself into?*

Switching to survivor mode, I threw up my hands in surrender. A dim light flickered overhead. *What was that?* I waited and watched. It happened whenever I raised my arms. I repeated the action, hands overhead, and again there was a faint glimmer. *Did I do that?* I lifted my left arm alone. Nothing. I tried my right arm, holding it high. And there was a light, brightening as if there were a flashlight in my hand, but only when my hand was elevated. *What was this?*

In the dim light, I saw that I was penned in a cell complete with bars. Quickly I shouted, "Liberty for All," figuring that if this was part of the game, it might work because that's what was on my card.

I heard a click, and the door swung free. With my right hand held high, I hurried down the corridor looking for the door back to the stairwell. I was hell-bent on getting out of there. I'd had enough. I couldn't remember how many flights I descended, but I would be happy to see florescent lights again. I opened the door.

Only the door didn't lead to the stairs. The room was fully-lit, and the Neanderthal sat at a table among other costumed players. There was Wonder Woman, Snow White, a Jedi, a Storm Trooper, the Doctor, and a spat-shoed Mr. Peanut. I hadn't seen him in years. But right in front of me was the most beautiful costume. A woman dressed as the Statue of Liberty, her face burnished copper, a torch in her right hand, and the elaborate folds of her tarnished green gown. Mr. Peanut interrupted my gaze when he yelled, "Take your seat, Lady Liberty, it's your turn."

I looked back to the woman and realized I was viewing my reflection. *Where did this costume come from? Was it a hologram?* I shrugged off my concerns and stood taller. Then I took my seat at the table. Gaming was never before this thrilling.

Connie J. Jasperson lives and writes in Olympia, Washington. A vegan, she and her husband share five children, eleven grandchildren and a love of good food and great music. She is active in local writing groups, and participates annually in NaNoWriMo. Music and food dominate her waking moments and when not writing or blogging she can be found reading avidly.

Find more of her work at https://www.conniejjasperson.com

CHARLOTTE

Connie J. Jasperson

Seated at his console in the control booth looking down on the robotics bay, Jason looked at his wrist phone. He wished he'd turned his earpiece off before sitting down to work, but he'd been expecting a call from a supplier. Charlotte's voice had been strange even for her, quiet and trembling. That could have been the drugs, but it upset him, as she must have known it would.

He hated the feeling of indecisiveness, wanted to ignore her plea. It should be so easy to walk away, simple to make that clean break he knew he should. Charlotte's primal need to be loved by everyone drove her to the arms of others, and they always let her down. She only returned to him whenever she had been destroyed.

It hurt, but not for the obvious reason. It hurt because she was damaged, and the predators knew it. Charlotte ran toward danger, never to safety.

Jason watched the screens but couldn't concentrate. She was down on Ballard Bay at the Upper 15th Street Mall, penniless and desperate.

"Jason? Did you read any kind of response?" Morty, short for Mortimia Radnor, was suited up and in the sterile lab with their newest creation. "I saw no visible reaction, but what did the EEG say?"

He glanced at his screens. "There was a spike, so he recognized the cup, but for some reason, he can't reach out and grasp it. Hey, sorry. I have to go downtown—a little family problem. Let's pick this up tomorrow, right?"

"Whatever. We aren't getting anywhere anyway." She sighed, a habit that aggravated Jason. "Your circuitry is good. The processor is working perfectly. I think the problem is in the micro hydraulics. I'm gonna tear him down tonight. I've got nothing better to do anyway. Go rescue your wife."

"Ex-wife."

"Whatever. You aren't done with her, so you're still married even if she isn't."

That was the way his and Morty's conversations about Charlotte usually went. After fifteen years they had established a comfortable rut, at ease with their separate yet together lives. He and Morty could drink beer, watch football, and tear down a robot with the best of them. She was his closest friend and lover, but they rarely discussed the reason they kept separate condos.

Charlotte.

Jason turned off the lights, locking the inner door behind him. He went down the back stairs to the parking garage, stepping out on the ground floor level. As he left the stairwell, a gust of wind snatched the outer door from his grasp, slamming it shut with a thunderous bang.

The noise of it felt like an omen. Charlotte calling out of the blue…the door slamming….

The last time he and Morty had come close to quarrelling, it had been about Charlotte. Morty said it was time for him to close the door on the past. Her words haunted him; she was right, but he couldn't let go of the dream. He hung on to his vain hope because of the memories, the whispers of a time when his ex-wife had been naive and full of joy, grasping at life.

The most popular girl at their college, Charlotte had bowled him over. He'd found her crying in the cafeteria. Overcome by the need to protect her, to make her happy again, he'd courted her in his awkward way. No one was more surprised than him when she eloped with him on a weekend fling in Vegas.

Why she selected the shy robotics major out of all the guys who vied for her, he never knew, but he didn't question it. The best year of his life… and at the age of twenty-two, he hadn't understood it would be so fleeting.

Jason walked across the garage, heading to rack four. His car had unracked and stood waiting for him. He pressed his thumb to the pad on the door, and it slid open. Leaning in, he quickly picked up small bits of gear and electronics from the front passenger seat, moving them to a box on the back seat, leaving plenty of room for Armando, Charlotte's yappy-dog. He emptied the trunk, as Charlotte never travelled light, even when homeless. He sealed the box and carefully covered it with a ratty beach-towel that had never seen a beach, tucking it in so Armando couldn't dislodge it if he got bored. He didn't want the dog to chew on something critical.

Maybe Armando no longer chewed on everything. The last time Jason had seen them, the dog was still a puppy, so maybe he was better behaved.

Jason climbed into the driver's seat, entering his destination and travel plan into King County Traffic Control. With the plan uploaded, the car soundlessly slipped out of the garage and wove its way through Bellevue. Too soon, it inserted itself into traffic on the third tier of I-405, linking into the chain.

Jason sat back, thinking, wondering why he was making such a stupid mistake. Charlotte came into his life like a soft breeze and left like a tsunami, leaving nothing but wreckage behind.

He had about twenty minutes until he arrived at the mall and used that time to decide what he wanted to do. If he took her back, she would be gone in three months, along with his self-respect and his savings.

Close the door on her. Walk away from the past.

Maybe he could get her into a detox unit. He couldn't just leave her downtown with the rest of the flotsam generated by an affluent society. She was incapable of living in an efficiency unit, despite the fact the cost-free shelter provided safety for those who were either down on their luck or unable to live in what passed for normal society.

Her voice had trembled when she told him she was trying to maintain sobriety. It always did when she lied, but she'd sounded sincere. Maybe so, it but wouldn't last long if she had to live downtown.

Swiveling the keyboard console toward him he accessed his bank, checking his available funds against what he needed to expend on the business. Not sure how long she would be around, he decided they would have to eat in rather than out. Charlotte was an expensive date.

He logged into his grocery account and filled out a pantry-box order. He also ordered a case of Armando's favorite dogfood. The drone would drop them at his condo in about an hour, and if all went well, Mercutio, his prototype android, would have them put away by the time he arrived home, making it appear as if he kept a well-stocked kitchen. Usually, he and Morty ate what passed for meals at the coffee-bar in the lobby of the building housing their small, currently profitless business.

That was assuming that Mercutio was functioning as he was designed. Four days previously, Jason had come home to find Mercutio had become jammed behind the kitchen door. And yesterday, he'd returned only to find his android had been scrubbing the downstairs toilet for most of the day. Hopefully, the new processor had resolved that.

Jason was fond of Mercutio regardless of his impending obsolescence. He had kept Jason sane when Charlotte had driven him mad. Other than Morty, the android was Jason's closest companion.

Laertes, the new prototype, was far more complicated, and already he showed a lot more initiative than Mercutio and his twin, Juliet, who had remained with Morty. Where the twins were far more complicated than the standard household bot, verging on the edge of self-awareness, they lacked the ability to think outside pre-programmed parameters. The cost of getting the rare metals for Laertes' components had beggared him and Morty for a year but was worth it.

Rescuing Charlotte would screw everything up. How could he get his ex-wife sober and keep his own sanity? If Charlotte was back in his life, how could he honor his financial commitment to Morty? And that was nothing next to his personal commitment. He loved Morty because she was everything Charlotte had never been—loyal, witty, soothing. She stuck with him despite Charlotte's ghost haunting their relationship. He didn't want to acknowledge how it must have hurt her.

A bitter thought, that.

He'd withheld a part of himself, saving it for a drug addict who would use him up and throw him away without a second thought.

Why couldn't he just cut the invisible cord that bound him to the memory of her?

It was time to stop berating himself and act decisively. His obsession was unfair to Morty. He wasn't fool enough to throw away everything he had built with her.

He focused on what he had to do first. Charlotte would open the conversation by telling him she was home for good. She would swear he was the only man she had ever really loved.

No. He wouldn't let it happen again. Morty deserved better than that.

Detox. That was the only way—get Charlotte into detox. Then he would figure out how to ease her out of his life.

Jason came back to awareness when he felt the slight bump and slowing that meant the car had unchained and now approached the mall entrance. It pulled up out front, waited while he got out, then left to go park itself.

For some reason, the big doors at the mall entrance had stopped working and were stuck shut. Jason waited in the growing crowd while the mech-bots did their job. It seemed like another sign telling him to turn back home and do as Morty wanted him to do. He should close the door on the past. He didn't need Charlotte's drama. The woman he'd loved so passionately had been dead for years—he just hadn't had a body to bury. He had his key out, about to recall his car when the doors suddenly swooshed open and the crowd carried him inside.

Jason entered the large, cool lobby area, but hung back, looking for Charlotte. He still hadn't decided what to do about her once he'd gotten her through the detox stage.

Then his gaze fell on the apparition that was Charlotte. It had only been four years since he'd last seen her, but she had aged at least twenty. For a moment he couldn't breathe. He leaned against a wall, thinking it couldn't be her, that Armando, ratty and in need of a bath, had wandered over to sit next to an old, worn-out whore in an act of random doggy kindness.

Charlotte was a wreck. She had made a pathetic attempt at putting on her make-up, which only served to give her gaunt features a clownish look. The once chestnut-brown hair he had loved so much still fell over her shoulders, but it had lost its luster, and instead of lush waves, her face was framed with thin, ropy strands the color of dirty ashes.

She was, as usual, dressed in shades of purple. She never wore any other color, but these tawdry bits of finery had been selected from the free clothing bins at some shelter. A large, floppy hat and a scarf disguised the angularity of her emaciated face but couldn't hide the physical evidence of a heavy pixie-dust addiction. Pixie-dust—such an innocuous name for the recreational drug the medical profession referred to as Satan's Sugar.

His girl-next-door had a Parkinson's-like tremor, a constant shaking of her head. Of course, she was vaping in public despite the glares of passing shoppers. Charlotte never obeyed rules.

Four years was all it had been since she left town with that guy she met in the gym. Four years of occasional emails from various places, saying "wish you were here." Four years of lies about her life, of her drug habit eating away at her.

His heart felt as if it had slowed to a stop, inundated with too many emotions to process. Denial, followed by a panicked frenzy of options spun through his mind. Too many thoughts, too much to say—his mouth couldn't form the words.

She had passed the tipping point, nearing the end of a long, slow, descent into organ failure. Her skin was pock-marked and jaundiced, the whites of her eyes a sickly yellow, and her teeth…oh god, those beautiful teeth….

The dog saw him first, lifting his head and wagging his tail. The look in Armando's eyes nearly broke Jason.

He knew.

The dog knew Charlotte had come home to die and he was terrified, wondering what would happen to him, and worried about her. Feeling as if he was in someone else's dream, Jason approached them, stooping down and patting Armando, who gazed up at him with pleading eyes.

Charlotte spoke first, surprising him. "He can't fix it this time, Armando." She raised rheumy eyes to Jason, and he winced. "I know. Don't say it, please."

Jason knelt by Armando, scratching the pooch's head. He tried to find words, any words, but they wouldn't come.

"I know I said I needed you to pick me up, but that's not exactly true. I've been in town for months. I've got a place nearby. I won't need it for long now, though." Her voice shook, raspy but decisive. "Look, I just need you to take care of Armando. He deserves better than this, and he loves you."

Jason finally managed to speak. "Why?"

"You and your eternal question of why." Charlotte barked a laugh, harsh and brassy. "I don't know. I've never known 'why.' Just accept the fact that it's my show and I'm going out my way. But I need to make sure Armando is okay before I go."

Jason exploded. "You expect me to take him away from you while you sit here? You expect me to drag this poor dog away, a dog who adores you, both of us knowing you're going to kill yourself?"

She took a drag on her e-cigarette, exhaling the vapor out the corner of her mouth. "Yes. That's exactly what I expect, and I know you'll do it. There's no turning back now for me. They don't waste time or money growing transplants for active addicts, and I'll never be anything else. Besides, it's too late for that. What's left of my body can't handle it. The medics all say I have weeks at the most, but probably less. I intend to go now, while I still have some shred of dignity."

Jason shook his head, willing the nightmare to go away. "You never could face reality, could you. You just couldn't live in the real world. You had to chase your fantasies, no matter who you hurt in the process. And look what it's done to you."

"I recognize reality when I see it. I think I'm facing it better than you are, robot-man."

Jason flinched at the old pseudo-affectionate term. She'd always claimed he was like his robots, devoid of emotions just because he was firmly grounded.

She patted his arm and stood up stiffly, like an old, old lady. Fishing around in her oversized handbag, she pulled out a small cloth sack, filled with lumpy things, which she handed to Jason. "These are his toys." She reached down and patted Armando. "Go with Jason. He loves us too."

Armando thumped his skinny tail and got to his feet. He picked his leash up in his mouth, looking up at Jason. Numbly, Jason took it.

"Go." Charlotte gave him a shove.

Dazed, Jason let Armando lead him toward the door. He turned back, in time to see Charlotte swiping her wrist phone across the meter, entering the cordoned off adults-only area where the sin-shops were located. She joined the group of freelance whores seated in the vaping section, men and women who were so far gone they were unable to find work even in the lower-class brothels. She stood waiting for the next john, blending right in, chatting with them like old friends.

A peculiar sense of finality settled in his heart as he realized she had walked out of his life forever, this time leaving him with a grieving dog to somehow care for.

The door had closed on him. Charlotte had acted decisively, closed and locked it against him.

The leash tugged in his hand, and he looked down, seeing loss and acceptance in Armando's eyes, and a desire to leave that place. Bending down, he picked the dog up.

He held Armando like a talisman against the pain, pressing his cheek against the dog's furry face. His voice was thick as he said, "Oh, god. We're both a mess. I wonder how you'll like Mercutio. You always hated the robovac." For some reason his vision had clouded; something burned his eyes.

A familiar voice said, "Want some help?"

He looked up; his face wet with tears he didn't know he'd shed.

Morty stood there, her expression one of concern. "She called me right after you left and said you and Armando might need a little company on the trip home. So, I called a cab." Awkwardly, she embraced him. "Look, I know you love her. I can live with that, but you need to let go of the past."

"You're right that I need to leave that behind. But I don't love her, that poor scarecrow of a woman wearing her skin. I love who she was twenty years ago, but that girl is dead and…and…she's never coming back, is she." Jason broke down, howling, sobbing into Morty's shoulder until his throat ached and he had no more tears.

"No. She's finally done the right thing." Morty held him, the depth of her understanding a refuge from the grief.

After a long moment, he pulled himself together, fighting the confused combination of relief and guilt. "I guess so. I stood there and did nothing, said nothing. I let her shut the door on the past while I stood dithering, trying to find the words to do it myself."

Morty looked sharply at him, then nodded. "It'll get easier."

Jason called his car, grateful for Morty's common sense and understanding. She reached for his hand. He felt the warmth of her grasp, of her presence. Morty had always been there and always would be.

As they walked into the hot, dry air of the passenger loading zone, he was stricken with the desire to look back, to see if Charlotte was watching him leave. He chose not to, instead waiting at the curb still holding Morty's hand, emotionally wrung but feeling an unaccustomed sense of liberty for the first time in years.

As if to make the break final, he heard the doors make an odd clunking noise as they whisked shut behind them. A woman's voice called, "Hey—why's the door not working?" She pressed the help bell, which was followed by the sounds of the mech-bots wheeling to the rescue. Once again, a crowd formed outside the broken doors.

Jason saw his car approaching and nuzzled the dog. "Guess what, Armando. I got you your favorite treats. And tomorrow you're going to spend the day at the doggy spa."

Armando licked his cheek.

Morty laughed. "He'll enjoy that. In fact, I could use a day at the spa myself. But fixing this glitch in Laertes comes first."

"Absolutely." Tears stung Jason's eyes but remained unshed. Working together for a common goal, building a real future with someone you could trust—Morty had always known what was important. That was what he appreciated most about her. She understood what love really was.

Thomas Gondolfi, father of three, gamer and loving husband, claims to be a Renaissance man and certified flirt. Raised as a military brat, educated as an electrical engineer, and having worked in many different fields has given him a unique perspective.

Tom has been writing fiction for over twenty-five years and doing it professionally for at least fifteen. He has six novels and dozens of pieces of short fiction in print. His most popular book by far is *Toy Wars*.

In 2012, he founded TANSTAAFL Press, which now publishes the works of three authors in a range of genres. You can find more of Thomas Gondolfi's work at www.tanstaaflpress.com

OPEN DOOR POLICY

Thomas Gondolfi

Moving should be a four letter word. That an auto-drive Uber held my belongings is a statement of sorts, but a man in my profession does better to travel light. I dump this load's last box of haphazardly packed stuff onto my desk. An abrupt crash announces one of my three coffee mugs breaking. At least it saves me from having to wash it, which is more than can be said about the laundry in the three trash bags sitting in the corner behind the door.

The heat of the summer winds along with a third-stage smog-alert might prompt even a sane person to walk purposefully under a landing airbus. Even the unions couldn't get their people to work in the marginally poisonous air and yet I had toted some forty boxes full of books up three flights of stairs.

Opposing the temperature outside, which would break sometime in September, the heat in my apartment will remain oppressive until I appease the landlady with four months of rent I don't have. A dearth of unfaithful husbands, missing persons, and deadbeat dads have my pockets temporarily empty. My sole contingency plan is collocating my home with my office.

I peel off my sweaty button-down and wipe the perspiration that had beaded on my head. A timid knock precedes two meters of unenhanced leg through my door. Timing isn't my strong suit.

"You Linc Thompson?" asks a sultry voice that could have gotten any stranger to strip just for the promise that she'd continue speaking.

"That's what's the door says, Miss," I say as I wipe my armpits. *In for a penny, in for a pound*, I think. I open one of the boxes and pull out one of my clean shirts to cover my sweat stained wife-beater.

The redhead steps in and around my junk with the grace and confidence of a runway model crossed with a professional gymnast. She eyes the seat piled with boxes. Her glance alone becomes a command. I race over and pick up the stack. "What can I do for you, Miss—?" I ask as I turn my head back and forth looking for a place to put my armload. When I find none, I toss them onto the bags of laundry.

"I'd like to hire you to do a job for me," she purrs, folding her skirt under her as she sits.

I didn't bother to tell her that any job I undertook would be expensive. Her designer outfit alone would pay my office and apartment rent for a year. I sit back down and pour myself a finger of scotch. I offer her the dollar store glass. She waves it away.

After I upend the drink I ask, "Cheating husband?"

She laughs melodically. "Not hardly, Mr. Thompson. I wouldn't get married. I like playing the field too much." Her brilliant green eyes skewer me. I look at her face closely for the first time. Her beauty doesn't stop with her curves. My crotch stirs uneasily. Everything about her says trouble but what a way to go down.

"OK, then what do you need me for? I can't imagine you need me to vet lovers."

Her lipstick chooses that moment to change from brilliant red to burgundy. "Not likely. No, I need your help with my sister."

"Did she go missing?"

"You aren't much of a detective, Mr. Thompson. You haven't gotten a single thing right yet."

It is my turn to laugh, and pour another finger of liquor. "I'm afraid we all have our prejudices, Miss—"

"My name is Janice Pollux. I'm worried about my sister. The last time I saw her she had a black eye and bruises on her neck and arms. She wouldn't tell me why."

I upend my second drink of the day. "Do you suspect anyone— husband, lover, drug dealer?"

"No, and that concerns me as well. She has a great marriage. Hell, she's even monogamous with her husband." Janice looks good even when she screws up her face with disgust. "She's a health nut as well. Won't touch alcohol or drugs."

"So all you want me to do is find out who is the problem?"

"And stop it."

"I can't guarantee the latter," I say, pouring another drink.

"I'm sure you will do everything possible," she says placing a stack of plastic bills on the desk between us. I play a mean hand of poker but I am hard pressed not to react to cash that will keep me for several months.

"I'll need her name, address, and universal number."

"Not a problem, Mr. Thompson. How soon can I expect some results?

§

Jennifer Francisco née Pollux and her husband live in a secure complex in the upscale Felida neighborhood of greater Portland. I've never understood why one group of soulless boxes is better than any other. Understanding the why of a thing doesn't matter as much as the practical application. A man lounging in a doorway in an upscale neighborhood is likely to be picked up by the local Metro Police on vagrancy, peeping, or even some trumped up charge. Well, technically peeping is what I am there to do, but not for any sexual satisfaction.

"Sir," says the automated voice of the Lyft. "Your waiting time is accumulating. At 11:33pm your charges have mounted to thirty-six dollars and fourteen cents." No one looks at anyone in a taxi. I'd already had four Metro drones pass by my location.

"Understand. Please continue to wait."

"As you wish, sir."

At the corner of 127th and 20th, the Fransiscos live on the sixty-third floor...all of the sixty-third floor. Alarm bells sound in my head, as if the forty thousand dollars Miss Legs dropped on me hadn't already pealed loud enough.

Using my magnifying contact lenses, the inside of the Fransisco home looks like a spread in Better Condos and Patios. The dining room has a Norman Rockwell lit by a Chihuly chandelier and a Wegner table and chairs. Hell, the yearly interest of the furnishings themselves would set me up for life in any non-extradition country of my choice. At least three boxed criminals, in mock maid prosthetics, scour the home. I whistle poorly around the Slim Jim I gnaw on.

Before I can peer into any more rooms, a baby-blue limo pulls up to the private landing. A couple exit the vehicle.

Friends ask me how I can tell so much from just a glance. It's easy after doing this job for a dozen years. It barely tickles my consciousness.

He wears a Kao Brothers suit, real silk tie, and Chinto Oxfords. A Maxine D'vorak, powder blue dress, which the limo had changed its color to match, accentuated her every curve. Giavito Rossi antique heels give her gams, even better than her sister's, a look that would entice a eunuch. You don't put on fancy duds to go to the supermarket. They also haven't been to the local pub because you don't bother with a limousine for such a pedestrian pursuit. So it had been a party of some kind.

That they are just back instead of on their way can be seen in the fact that neither of their hair styles are perfectly in place. She has a slight smear in her makeup across one cheek.

The way he hauls her out of the vehicle by one arm is likely to leave bruises on a stone statue. They come home before midnight when most sensible upwardly mobile corpies aren't caught dead leaving a social gathering before one A.M.

All the tiny things add up and flash into my brain as one—they are just back from a party that hadn't gone well and he either blames her or is taking it out on her—the difference only important to a judge.

I dial in my Sonic Ear on their location as the limo pulls away.

"…flirting like a fucking whore." *Lovely*, I think, *a jealous husband*.

"Steve, really I didn't do anything like that."

"So how did his lipstick get on your cheek? Don't deny it."

"It was—"

Sometimes I don't understand couples as they live intimately together and don't know how to read one another's posture, expressions, and moods. She certainly doesn't read his body language. I know what is coming before she opens her mouth. While his heavy-weight boxer size doesn't normally matter in any real fight, this is abuse and she isn't within three weight classes of him. His ten kilo fist drives her face backward like a sledgehammer. Her head bounces against the window behind her before she crumples to the ground.

"I said don't deny it, bitch."

"Stay down," I mutter only to myself. I wince as her head lifts up and she reaches for him.

"Steven, please. I—"

Grabbing her upraised arm to deny her a defense, the brute drives his fist into her face three more times in quick succession. Blood sprays her dress and the window as her nose explodes.

So much for a "good marriage." I have to stop this before she gets herself killed. "Lyft, please take me to sixty-third floor, twenty twelve, one hundred twenty-seventh street."

"I'm sorry, sir, but that is a private landing zone. Do you wish me to contact the owners for permission to land?"

"No, that's alright. Instead, take me to the sixty-fourth floor of the same address."

"Yes, sir." My cab lifts slightly and pivots across the street. I try to follow the massacre below me but the view is blocked by the body of the cab.

"We've arrived at your destination. Your fare is forty-six dollars even."

I ignore the cab jumping out. Behind me I hear. "Sir, unless you pay we will charge your universal number your fare plus a two hundred credit collection fee."

From my waist, I pull out a carabiner and fasten it to the railing. The climbing harness I wear under my clothes proves useful in almost every case. Drawing my Billy club, I jump the barrier, belaying at my waist and feeling the straps jerk tight into my crotch. The outward jump swings me pendulum like back down onto the sixty-third floor platform. The lack of immediate attack surprises me. Scanning quickly, I fumble to unhook my line. I see nothing of the husband. And a small heap on the ground emits a faint, regular whistling just above the snarl of the city.

My crepe sole shoes make no sound as I pad over to the heap, hooking my weapon back onto its loop on my belt. Her face looks three times its normal size. Both eyes are swollen shut and her nose has that askew look that, as a veteran of many bar brawls against jarheads, I can attest is broken. Every breath whistled around the blood that bubbled from her mouth and nose.

I trigger my percomm. While I might not be able to get a cab to land at a restricted platform, I certainly can call for one. "Call Uber."

"Would you like a ride, sir?" comes the automated voice.

"Yes. Now if not sooner," I say as I run my hand through her thick red hair to check her skull for fractures. The woman moans but doesn't open her eyes or speak.

"We have your location. Estimated arrival in one minute forty-three seconds."

I look at the front door and will it to stay closed for a bit more than a hundred heartbeats. I pick up the fifty kilos of battered meat.

"Uber arriving for Linc Thompson," the car announces. I provide the woman's limp wrist to the vehicle's DNA scanner. I need to create a false trail. I slide her inside and climb into the cramped Hyundai auto-drive. "Destination?"

"Voodoo Doughnuts."

"Thank you," the taxi offers.

The woman moans.

"Does your companion require medical assistance?"

"No thank you." I rip off one of my sleeves to gently mop the blood from her face. I chastise myself for saving the woman. I tear her lacy slip from under her dress and fashion a veil to cover her visible damage. I always get too involved. Sometimes I want to just have my heart removed so that I quite caring.

"Arriving at destination: Voodoo Doughnuts"

47

"Cancel. New destination: Lloyd Center, ground level."

At ground level I pay off the cab and carry her to the bus stop. In the dark, at ground level near bar closing, I am not surprised that there are others holding up someone unconscious or nearly so. When you want to be invisible, be with similar people or those too inebriated to notice a hippopotamus riding a bicycle.

We bus to Hillsboro's Wintel plant, Lyft to the Frank Estate Brothel, and pick up a pedicab to the worst area of ground level. I half drag and half carry my compatriot three blocks. Just off of Third Street, I pay cash for a double at Red Roof Inn. Sliding her inside and crawling into the one by two by three meter tube room I decide that my job of obfuscation wouldn't fool a dedicated sleuth but that I'd bought some time.

§

"Steven?" slurs a voice that wakes me up in the coffin-like room.

"Nope," I say. Black and blue eyes remain sealed shut by swelling and an oozing ichor. "Linc. Relax, you're safe. Your sister hired me to protect you from your husband."

"No hus'and," she garbles between two badly split lips.

"Huh, wasn't Steven your husband?"

"'oyfriend." Her hands go up to her face.

"Careful, your face is a mess right now. You'll heal but it'll take time. But let's get back to you. Aren't you Jennifer Pollux?" In the tiny pull-out sink I wet a washrag and used it to dab at the crustiness around her eyes. She flinches but lets me clean her.

"Susan 'oylan."

Congratulations, dickhead. You saved the wrong woman.

"Did you know Steven is married?"

"Yes. Lea'ing his 'ife."

"OK. Do you still want him after what he did to you?"

She takes long enough that I think she may have passed out. "I got no'ody else."

"Well, from what I see you can have your choice of men, I suggest a change."

"Thank you 'ut I not so 'retty no'."

"Wait until we get you put back together."

"'hy are you hel'ing 'e?"

"Because I care. I have to go out for a bit—"

"Don't go."

"I'll be back. I need to decide where we can go next to throw off any pursuit." *And figure out where I messed up*, I think to myself.

§

"Have you saved my sister yet," Janice says over the percomm. Her hair, rucked up in a red and black beehive, distracts me for a moment.

I call from a Starbucks in Kelso, just to make sure if I'm traced it won't lead back to Susan. "Sorry, Janice, no. I have – "

"That's disappointing, Mr. Thompson." Her head turned to address someone off screen. "No, the black on my nails."

"Ms. Pollux, you said that your sister is monogamous. What about her husband?"

"Steven? That worm? He'd fuck anything that didn't move out of the way of his dick."

"Does Jennifer know about her husband's…infidelities?"

"Yes. She know he fools around."

"Does she know about specific partners?"

"Doubt it. She never mentioned any of them. She doesn't care. She know he can't get enough but he always comes back to her."

"OK, what if there were a chance he might not come back?"

Janice jerks her head around to look right into the percomm. Her perfectly formed eyebrows knit together. "She probably would claw the chippie's eyes out and then sew her snatch shut."

"Thank you, Ms. Pollux. I think I can proceed from here."

§

"Who's there?" Susan says, trying hard to open her blackened eyes.

"Stay still. It's just Linc," I say, sliding back into the tube room. "Susan, have you ever met Steven's wife?"

"'itch! I tol' her to get out 'ecause Ste'en is 'ine. 'e had a 'ight."

"When was that?"

"T'o 'eeks ago."

That accounts for the bruises Janice mentioned.

"One more question. What happened tonight? Why did Steven beat you up?"

She rolls onto her side to face me, wincing as she does. One eye barely cracks open. "He thought I 'as hitting on his 'artner."

Asking her about whether Steven really plans on leaving his wife isn't going to give me any value. She focuses only on what she wants to see. I need to talk to Steven.

"We need to move you. Now that you can walk we should have no problem."

§

After several preparations, not the least of which is a bottle of vodka, I return to my office. If Steven has any interest in tracking Susan he will find me here. Kicking up my feet on my desk, I pour myself a stiff drink.

As I suspect, two drinks later, Steven slams his way into my tiny office, shattering the opaque, bullet-proof window inset, and smashing the deadbolt through the frame. What surprises me is that he is in full Portland Metropolitan Police uniform. Mentally, I curse myself in six languages for being seven kinds of fool and getting involved in this case. Had I even suspected the Metros were involved I wouldn't have touched it with a ten meter pole covered with three condoms and a repulsion spell. The chance of seeing even another dime in fees drops to zero. I bless my paranoia in my preparations.

"Steven Francisco, I presume."

"And you are Linc Thompson. I guess we don't have much to hide from one another. Give me one reason not to kill you right now."

"I'll give you two, actually. First, if you kill me you will never learn of the location of Susan. And second, as you are not in riot gear, the concussion of the bomb under your feet will kill you just as dead as I would be. I don't take you for a man who will trade his life just to get mine."

"It seems we have something of a stalemate…for now," he barks from behind his black uniform.

"Not exactly, Officer Francisco. As corrupt as the Metros are, I don't think they will take kindly to having the footage of your landing pad publicized along with the testimony of your Mistress. I'm quite adept with electronics." I pour myself another glass trying to make sure my hands remain steady. Threatening a police officer ranks right up there with sleeping with a cobra.

"If you do, nothing will stop me from killing you."

"I don't doubt it. I could give you the names of at least three hundred individuals who'd take the job for less than ten grand, unless you wanted the satisfaction yourself. So the standoff is somewhat permanent."

"You mess in my domestic affairs and want me to just walk away? I think you need to check on that liquor you are drinking. I could torture the files and her location from you."

"Under normal circumstances, I'm sure you could but I don't know where either are. I can't give you what I don't know."

He growls and delivers a menacing Metro stare.

I tilt the glass his way and smile. "Here is the deal. You never look for, talk to, or interact with Susan ever again, and the platform videos disappear into my personal archives, along with the proof of aliens, and Bigfoot photos. In addition, you leave me alone. With the cash I gave her, Susan should be able to make it to any number of extradition free countries completely without a trace." I leave off the alternative as too obvious to state.

"You know there will come a time when one of you two will slip up. When that happens, you are both dead."

"I'm sure of it, Officer Francisco, but that day is not today.

"Now if you would be so kind, I'm choosy about my drinking companions. Not only that but I'm also going to need to find someone to repair my door."

I pour myself another drink. Picking up the glass, I look around as I shoot it. The big black piece of *merde* is gone.

I'm a sucker. Susan got almost all of Janice's cash. She needs as much as I could give her to make it out of this country. I held back about enough for a new window and a month's rent, but then with a Metro bounty hanging over me I wonder if either would be worthwhile.

It looks as if I've trapped myself well and truly good this time. I pour myself another drink. I am alive and have at least a modicum of a head start. Maybe I need not to just fix another doorway, but find an entirely new door.

Maybe life as a terrorist would be safer.

Liam R.W. Doyle has been a member of NIWA for over three years and this is his third story to be included in the organization's anthologies. He moved to Portland, Oregon virtually on a dare, and to his utter lack of surprise, discovered he never wants to live anywhere else. While he has yet to become a true outdoorsman, he has gotten used to rain without an umbrella. Liam has several short stories, and the novel *Singularity Deferred*, available, and you can find out more at www.tragic-sans.com

TORRENTIAL

Liam R.W. Doyle

"I'm almost back," Christine says to the unintelligible voice that is now ever-present but tuned down to a mumble. As if it knows, understands, and has accepted being patient a little while longer. Christine, however, is impatient, and stands at the edge of the campus, staring out at the rolling, sunburnt hills that stretch away from the city. Endless wrinkled land in mottled tans and grays, grasses and rock that expand from the Cascades east to the horizon. She sees the top of the sun just start to pour like molten metal over the crest of a hill. The forecast calls for a cool winter day for Bend, likely high of only 30 Celsius. Fortunately, where she is going today, the sun and its dry oven heat won't reach her.

The crunch of steps on gravel behind her draws her attention. Dr. Javier Garza, adjunct professor and junior researcher for the Portland Project, and her assigned pilot and chaperon, has come to meet her. His smile is too friendly for the morning and she hopes he won't be talkative on the trip.

"I hope you like sandwiches. With the kitchen there closed this week, I brought a variety in case you didn't pack anything," he says, holding up one of the two nylon duffles he's carrying. Her hopes for a quiet trip dwindle.

"I'm good," she says.

Garza nods and tosses his packs in the craft's cabin. "All set?" he asks as he climbs in after them. Christine nods and gets in without another look at the desert scenery. The VTOL aircraft's electric rotors lift the craft slowly, silently, before tilting and banking west toward the mountain pass that will lead them to the Portland Peninsula. Christine hopes she can nap for the hour it will take. Although, even if not kept awake by Garza, her own memories and visions will likely keep her awake—just as they have kept her increasingly awake for months. Visions of black skylines she can't quite make out, of shadowy long-limbed creatures. The voice, on the other hand, has become almost soothing, susurrant, of late.

Shortly after passing through the Cascades, they enter the Willamette wetlands consisting of thousands of acres of swamp and marsh. They fly over a spider webbing of creeks and streams interspersed with patchy green foliage. "Forests and vineyards," Garza says, as if continuing a conversation Christine wasn't aware she was a part of.

"Sorry?"

"Back when the city was here, before the change, all this used to be forests and vineyards. Can you believe it? Trees hundreds of feet tall!"

"My family owned a vineyard," she says before remembering she doesn't want to contribute to conversation.

Garza looks over at her. "Really? Out here?"

She shrugs, committed to the conversation now. "Long ago, of course. Twenty…twenty-first century." She is realizing now she has not thought about family. Not in a while. Not much since last year.

She had been close with her family, until recently. She tries not to think about why that has changed, but there is no denying it. They have been trying harder to reach her lately and she is avoiding them, partly from preoccupation—her conscious excuse. But, she senses, she is anticipating a coming, longer separation. Something permanent.

The voice, though she doesn't understand the words that it says, has nonetheless imparted that message, that feeling to her. The voice that started speaking to her that day a year ago. The voice that she at first questioned if real, naturally, but has since accepted it sharing space in her head. Since doing that, the voice has been a lot less…insistent, more urging than commanding, if unintelligible to her.

"Anything left of it? Have you been there?"

She starts, shaken out of the reverie she had fallen so quickly into, then chuckles despite herself. "Sorry," she says and continues, "from what we have of records, it was between Portland and the coast…the old coast, somewhere. I did try to find something of it when I came here the first time, a year ago." After a pause, her voice becomes more measured. "Of course there's nothing now. Just marshes."

"Would have been nice to have found even a building, huh? That's what you photograph anyway, yeah?" Garza asks. "Undersea buildings?"

Christine shrugs. "Sort of. Any submerged pre-deluge architecture. I got most of the bridge ruins last time." She blinks away an image of Gothic arches imposing on her thoughts.

"We'll be flying just past the tip of one of them shortly. And the old city center buildings." Garza falls silent then and they fly the last several minutes with only the sound of wind and electric turbines.

Soon, the wide river they follow opens up into a sea and, in the distance, Christine sees the ridge of hills that form the Portland Peninsula. In front of the cliffs, drawing closer, are vague smudges that quickly take shape and form a copse of several buildings sitting placidly in the water, incongruous with the otherwise complete lack of human civilization around them. They are the top handful of floors of ancient skyscrapers, most of them empty of windows. Vines and moss climb up their sides and carpet the edges and corners as if the sea itself was reaching up with vegetation to try to pull these few stubborn structures, standing against the ravages of time, down to join the graveyard of collapsed and decaying things.

She has been seeing a decaying, otherworldly skyline in her dreams. She had thought perhaps old, pre-deluge Portland. But she has found pictures of what it once looked like and, while not the skyline of her dreams, something about it, the silhouette of that old city, the impression, tugs at her. Even now, fully awake, she can almost see the dreamscape superimposed on the actual ruin they approached. There is something about what she sees in her mind's liminal space that reminds her of that old city. Not exactly, but rather a twisted and melting, literally breathing, version of a city. She cannot fathom how or why her mind would invent such a landscape. She knows it is connected to the voice in some way.

They fly by the tops of a pair of bridge towers with broken and slack suspension cables hanging off them to disappear into the water. Christine's stomach tightens at seeing it, actual memories of last time playing at the edges of her mind.

"Looks like high tide," Garza says, "but you can see the tops of another set that way, north of here. Parts of three of the bridges still stand. St. John's farther up's still whole, actually."

Christine nods appropriately and bites back the urge to tell him she saw that last time. She continues to watch the nearby rusted and corroded bridge tower in the wind rippled water until it passes far behind them.

Garza banks the craft and flies toward the Tualatin Cliffs rising from the Columbia Sea. He flies low above the water, along the tree-covered rocks. Christine looks out and sees bits and pieces of stone peeking out from the scattered foliage. It's not immediately obvious what they are, but she recognizes them as building foundations, roads, fences, and other remnants of the civilization that used to live on these hills, centuries ago, before the face of the planet changed. Before plagues and famine and migrations.

Looking at these ruins, Christine feels an odd disconnect, a lurch in her consciousness. They are not nearly as ancient as Roman or Greek or Egyptian ruins, but for all intents and purposes, no less so either. The people that lived here, in the 21st century, were more similar to her and her world now than they were to the Romans. But she feels no less distant from those doomed people of Portland than she does from the people of Pompeii. Part of her understands the ruins she sees passing below her is a reminder of how close all of humanity came to disappearing, but part of her can't help but feel removed from it to the point of apathy. She may have had ancestors who lived here when it was still a thriving metropolis, but did the people with Italian heritage who visited Rome feel any particular kinship with the people who built the Colosseum?

Garza follows the cliff line until an opening in the hills reveals itself and he turns into the inlet. They come quickly to a modern building and pier sitting on the mountain river. The building itself bears no marking but a holographic overlay on the VTOL windscreen tells Christine they're approaching Pittock Pier. Garza lowers the craft to a pad next to the building and an older man with a long but perfectly manicured gray beard comes out to greet them.

"Doctor Garza, welcome back. I wasn't expecting you until the new semester," the man says as he checks the connection on the induction charger for the VTOL.

Garza hands Christine her bag as he pulls out one of his. "Hey, Paul. Escorting our guest here. Paul, Christine Mason, artist and scholar. Christine, this is Paul. One of the Project techs in residence out here."

"You live here," Christine says, shaking Paul's hand.

"Half the year. There's a lot of the old structure that used to be here down below us. Some of it's been renovated into labs and apartments for faculty and researchers, and whatnot," he nods, indicating Christine. "Stays cooler in the summer that way." He gestures to the building they can see above ground, "That's mostly just boats and stuff."

Garza grabs his bag and starts walking to the plain building, gesturing to Christine to follow along. "We're here for a couple days. Do you want to check it out now or get going?"

"Let's get started. Please." Christine shoulders her own bag, leaving Paul all but forgotten.

Within an hour, Christine is changed into her wetsuit and standing on the pier waiting for Garza to join her. She ties her hair back and wipes sweat off her forehead. It's cooler here than around Bend by maybe a few degrees but more humid. More tropical than the arid desert just on the other side of the mountains, and here she smells the heavy scent of ocean water.

She flexes her bare toes and feels the patina of slimy algae under her feet. For a moment, her defenses are lowered and she recalls the feeling of slimy tendrils of seaweed wrapped around her ankles a year ago, pulling her down. It couldn't have been pulling her down, she knows that. Part of her still clings to that. But she also knows that it was. She knows she shouldn't be here, shouldn't be alive, shouldn't be standing on this pier. She should still be out there, desiccated bones among the weeds and ruins in the brackish water.

"I take it you know the subski well?" Garza says, startling her, making her choke back a shout.

She nods her head a little too emphatically and watches him walk past in his wetsuit, also barefoot, to the end of the pier. She's brought back to the sensation of the slime under her own feet, suppresses a shiver, and moves quickly but gingerly back to her equipment to get her flippers on.

It's curious, she thinks, how the water takes what it wants. Out there, the flooded and half-buried city of long ago. And here, on this modern pier, built within the last decade or two, the water is trying to claim it as well. Algae, slime, the persistent layer of green life, growing and demanding. Age after age, eon after eon. Before us, after us, she thinks, despite us.

She joins Garza where the pair of subskis are moored. While checking the indicators on each one, Garza says, "There's some tourists or other out east of here, according to Paul. Otherwise, not much going on today. Well, that and the chance of heavy rain this afternoon."

"Oh?" Christine says, half interested, as she straps the aerator onto her back. The subski creates a bubble of air around the pilot's head and torso, but for both safety and swimming beyond the subski, the ultra-light SCUBA equipment is still necessary.

"Yeah," he says, moving to his own equipment, "we should keep an eye on it. Probably'll be nothing, but you know how it is around here."

She doesn't know but nods anyway.

Within minutes the two of them are lying on their stomachs on the subskis, bobbing in the water. "Okay, Mx. Mason," Garza says, his voice coming to her from both him and her earpiece, creating a distracting disconnect, "This is your project, you're in charge. I'll guide you around anything dangerous, but I'm mostly going to just hang with you in case. Buddy system."

"Right," Christine says, giving her facemask one last wiggle. In a rare moment of levity she blames entirely on nerves, says, "try to keep up." She throttles and angles the sleek craft downward and is hit with an initial spray of water. The cool river envelops her body briefly before the craft is deep enough for its positive pressure envelope to surround her torso with a pocket of air generated by extracting gases from the water itself. She pushes down the immediate panic reflex as she takes her first breath while underwater.

No matter how many times she has used subskis since she was a girl growing up around the Arizona Bay, her brain never wants to believe the mixed signals she gets from the rest of her body that she is underwater, yet can still breathe. It's not like SCUBA diving, where having something in her mouth or directly over her face seems to convince her brain there isn't anything odd about breathing in water. Having nothing but a few inches of empty air between her face and the water that would like nothing more than to rush in and drown her, will always be disconcerting, she knows. With a mouthpiece, she feels, the water concedes the battle. It agrees to remain passive, letting her swim through and with it, not willing to harm her. On a subski, she feels the battle between her and death every second, waged at the molecular line between air and water.

She lets the subski idle, gliding gently forward while she centers herself. She focuses on a blurry, wavering boulder in the water before her, paying attention to the feeling of the water on her legs, the sound of the electric motor and the air generator, the fresh yet fishy smell of river water.

She becomes more aware that Garza is idling near her, silent. She wonders if he's also going through his own acclimation process. No, she decides, he's the kind of guy who can probably just tell she needs the moment and is giving it to her. What would have, a moment ago standing on land, made her feel unnecessarily irritated at him for his consideration, she is now grateful for. She wonders about how the transition from air to water can change her outlook, demeanor, perspective so quickly and noticeably. The cooperation with the water, the belonging, the curiosity she feels is her natural state. The fear is an imposition.

She is impatient with herself, even if Garza is not. "Ready," she says, her voice distorted in the bubble envelope and increasing her unease. She throttles forward and glides through the water, Garza following close behind.

They exit the river and return to the sea, the long-dead city slowly emerging from the gloom and revealing itself around them. The water, a brackish mixture of freshwater runoff from the rivers coming out of the mountains, and ocean water, is clear enough that she can see the hundred or so feet below her to the crumbled and decaying ruins on the seabed floor. Sunlight dances and moves through the water over the landscape like a living, physical thing. As Christine glides forward, silent but for the whine of the envelope generator, objects manifest from the gloom at the edge of her vision, wavering and distorted from the lensing effect of the divide between air and water. Ghosts of buildings, darker green in the dark green murk, waver. Christine's stomach churns and she shivers. What she is seeing evokes the visions she has been given.

The map info pulled from centuries-old data is displayed on the subski's screen inches in front of her face, depicting a terrain that no longer exists. Depicting lines that are roads among stores and apartments, that are in reality vague separations between collections of piles of debris. She follows a map that a few centuries ago she might have used to drive an automobile around town, and imagines herself a dot on the animated clean line between the stark squares. One of many dots as hundreds, thousands, of other people used similar maps in similar vehicles doing similar things. That is the world the digital map scrolling on the display promises. Streets that had names. Buildings that had purpose. Pretending the decaying reality she glides over is that lost world. A memory in the mind of someone lost to dementia.

The display indicates a library below. She glides over concrete slabs and pillars. The display wants her to see an arena. She looks down to see a ragged horseshoe of stadium seats around a field of seaweed. The display wants her to follow a highway. She strains to trace a shattered ribbon cutting through the ruins.

The display tells her that her goal is not far ahead. She peers through the bubble's membrane, watching the mottled and sunbeam-infused water for the structure she sees in dreams, in images that come to her when her mind wanders, found in patters of textures her mind rearranges to resemble. And soon it melts out of the murk and takes shape before her. The Gothic cathedral arches of the St. John's Bridge. The bridge defies reason by still being whole. The suspended length of it reaches out into the gloom, over an undersea ravine that used to be a river. The steel towers rise higher still and burst forth above the surface of the sea. She already knows what the tops of the spires look like from her previous visit, the massive cables sloping from their apex.

She remembers the impossible creature that clung to them, watching her, before clambering down the steel cables to disappear into the water before she could acknowledge what she saw was real.

"Storm's picking up."

She's startled into jerking on the throttle and lurches the subski forward. She had completely forgotten she wasn't alone, the subski's bubble creating a private pocket universe. "What?"

"Surface winds already thirty kilometers an hour," Garza says.

She cranes around to see his shimmering subski close behind her.

"How long have we been down here?"

"About an hour."

Christine scowls. It feels like both minutes and years. Time doesn't exist down here. "I…haven't even begun yet."

There is a pause. Then, "We're okay if we stay deep, but if the coastal watch sees lightning, we need to get back. We can't go deep enough here to avoid a lightning strike. Wait for it to pass and try again. We have a couple days, after all. "

"Fine," she says dismissively and angles the subski down toward the base of the pylons—toward the flowing tendrils of plants that a year ago wrapped themselves around her legs as she dived to follow the creature. She slows the subski to a gentle glide, letting inertia bring her closer. She notices Garza lazily moving on, presumably leaving her to her work and realizes she hasn't even made a pretense yet of activating the cameras.

The sickly yellow-green leaves dance and sway, performing a sensual routine around the base of the bridge. Here since the flood. Here since before the flood, when it was a river. Here, hidden beneath the people and the cars and the boats and civilization for the eyeblink of time between when this was indigenous Chinookan land and then no longer land at all. It was here as the freshwater was invaded by salt, adapting, changing in order to live but never changing in purpose. To claim for the water. And, she knows, it hides the creature.

And the creature guards the doorway.

She doesn't know how she knows that. Probably the same way she's been called by it for the past year. Called back to it. Seen it in her dreams, the eyes. The voice that's not a voice. The curtain of weeds parting for her, caressing her in her dreams. Eventually, in her wakefulness. While talking at a gallery show, listening at a conference, eventually sitting at her kitchen table for days in a row—feeling the long caress, the wrapping, the pulling across the distance no matter where she went.

Christine is barely aware of Garza's voice in her ear, "It's getting worse up there, we need to head back."

The damned bubble is making it hard to see. She pulls the ultra-light SCUBA mouthpiece off the Velcro on her chest, puts it in her mouth and the flow instantly starts. She pushes off the subski and the envelope of air collapses. Her ears pop, and her facemask presses against her skin and everything around her is suddenly clear. She breathes in. Being now part of the water, truly inside it, ironically makes the act of breathing through the regulator easier, more natural, than breathing in the bubble.

The subski drifts nearby, LiDAR-sensing her position and never allowing itself to get too far from her. But she has already forgotten it. She scissors her legs, keeping position in front of the curtain of mottled green. It is turning gray—the light is fading. The storm is arriving. Darkness presses in.

"Mason, Christine, seriously, I can't let you stay here. We need to head back now." She sees the light from his subski cut swaths through the murk over her. Then he is forgotten again.

She knows it is watching her. She sees its eyes. Its many eyes, that congeal into two pairs, then one pair. Behind the leaves she can barely see now. But she sees the eyes.

She drifts closer. The long fingers of leaves curl and bend toward her. They touch her, tease at her, gentle and eager, no longer needing to grasp and wrap and pull like a year ago when she was taken by surprise, panicked, fought against it. It knows she wants to be here, needs to be here now. She knows this, but she doesn't know why.

The creature pulls itself out of the concrete pylon to separate itself as a distinct being apart from the bridge. Its arms are long, longer than its body by three or four times, and drifting down to the sea floor. They wave and flow like the weeds still between Christine and it.

Garza is saying something but she no longer hears. She is barely aware of him circling above her, around her discarded subski. The creature pulls its arms up like it is reeling them in, until the hands wrap around her entire body. The fingers, with dissolving boundaries fading into the water around them, wrap around her once, twice, three times. They are translucent, she sees the weeds and the eyes and the bridge through the smoke hands— clearer, in fact, since the storm stole the sun above. But she hears Garza in her ear, urgent, calling for her, unable to see her any longer. She feels ensconced in an embrace by the creature, but experiences no resistance to stop her reaching up and removing the earpiece. She lets it and Garza's voice drop to join the disintegrating artifacts from a lost culture.

How many, she wonders. How many cultures has the creature seen. And she feels the answer, she doesn't simply know it or see it as through its own eyes like a replaying of memory, for the creature does not always have eyes. She feels the recent centuries of loneliness, and ghosts, and then the people, the masses of people all around, everywhere. And in reverse, she feels the people, and the spirits they brought with them from other lands, thin and scatter. And then she sees the people who spoke to the land. The people that spoke to the creature. Feared and worshiped it in equal measure. Centuries of them, living by the river. Living by the doorway. The door that was there then and further back, before the first people. Before even the spirits. Before the land stopped being molten liquid. Before there was anything to be seen or touched in this cluster of dark matter in space.

The doorway she is being invited through…

That she is ready, this time, to pass through…

That she can already see in her mind, through the creature's mind, seeing without eyes.

A different kind of land, and on it, a different kind of city. Not of buildings as she has any concept of them, but living creatures of membrane and sinew that form a patchwork landscape. And infesting this organic world are other living things, ones that despite seeing them with the creature's senses, are so impossible for her mind to comprehend, they are translated into her brain as vibrating blurs and moving smears on her vision. The world she sees is inverted, concave, folded over on itself in a geometry that makes her ill trying to understand it—knowing she is not even seeing a fraction of what is there. Even so, she is seeing, clearly, finally, what has been teasing at her mind for months.

In the center of this malformed city, on a hill made of flesh and algae, towers a figure her mind wants to categorize as human, covered in tattered swaths of yellow cloth. It, he, speaks to her, through the creature, and she knows it is not a memory of the creature's, but what is really there, happening, beyond the doorway. The figure in yellow tells her, in thoughts she understands though she hears the gibbering language of the voice, that it ends. Is ending. And she must come. She is to join with him, as many like her have done through the past—but she is the last. She is the last to come through, and with her crossing, the doorways—here and elsewhere—will no longer be necessary. And already, she knows her mind has crossed through, and even if somehow she were to say no, she would not come… her mind, twisted, would still remain until her body withered on Earth.

Yes, she says.

And then she is back in her body and feels the shockwave through the water as the impossibly huge cables snap and give way from the towers. As if they have been holding on, tenuous and earnest, these last few centuries for just this moment to let go. The support gives, the deck falls as all the energy holding the steel pieces into recognizable shape releases and it crumbles into the ruin below in torrential surge and chaos of water. She feels dirt and debris and currents move violently around her, but she is held immobile and placid by the creature, still in its evanescent grip.

A distant part of her remembers Garza, wonders if he had given up the search for her and gone back or had still been around and is now surely lost to the destruction. She knows it won't matter.

She sees the tower before her, monochromatic, shades of black as it rises above her, alone and no longer tethered to anything, rising above the surface of the water still roiling with both the bridge collapse and the storm. She sees the tower above the water as clearly as she sees the tower in the water before her, as if there no longer is any water at all, or rather, no barrier, optical or otherwise, between the two states of matter.

The world arcs and tilts away. She realizes it's the tower, and it is falling away from her. Separating from the roots anchoring it below ground, as if sheared off at the seabed, and falling slowly. The shades of black becoming shades of silver then photo-negative as lightning strikes in long continuous arcs around her. The tower falls into the water, through the ebony murk, onto the rubble and into the ground. The framework of cathedral arches that gave the tower of the St. John's Bridge its silhouette, continues through the ground like a hot wire through Styrofoam, cookie-cutting its shape into the ancient rock, leaving giant cathedral-arched holes of absolute black.

This is the doorway. She knows it has always been here since the steel and technology, since the spirits and the lodges, since the ancient gods, since the nothing that was always. She is not the first, she understands this. Some have passed through the doorway, in other ways, for millennia, but she will be the last. Something is coming, something that has waited, eons for this world but only a moment for that which has slept.

She is no longer being held by the creature, the guardian. It waits. It drifts and is broken and reformed by the movement of the water. Christine swims forward. She is no longer breathing through the regulator—there isn't one. No mask, no wetsuit. She is naked and does not know when or how, but does not care. They are no longer needed. She swims, her form black on black, to the holes carved into the earth. Into the void revealed by fallen steel.

EM Prazeman is the author of twin trilogies The Lord Jester's Legacy and The Poisoned Past, as well as various short stories published in the nooks and crannies of the kind of anthologies that often aren't very well-behaved. Additionally, she's written the pagan afterlife novel *After* as KZ Miller and a memoir, *House of Goats*, as Tammy Owen. Her husband Rory Miller is also an author. They have two remarkable adult children and a small farm in the Pac NW. For more information visit emprazeman.com.

WARMTH

EM Prazeman

Bethmay heard him tromping through the wintry woodland, his breath softly sawing in the otherwise still air. Eventually she saw him among the bare, dark trees, using a walking map to guide him to the meeting place she'd set up. His head bowed beneath a heavy hood worn over a cloak of dark wool, and tall leather gaiters kept his trousers as dry as possible and the snow out of the tops of his heavy-soled boots. He carried both a sword and two pistols. That was wise, considering the creatures that hunted these woods. Like her, the dragons and bears spent most of their time sleeping, but some flesh eaters hunted even now.

She decided to spare him the extra miles toward the broad slopes of the flat-topped mountain on which she lived in summer and emerged from beneath the shelter of the white-capped boughs of an evergreen. Without the interruption she might have slept there for days, maybe even a week. The more waking time she allowed herself in winter, the more she had to hunt. Hunting was dangerous, exhausting, and put an added burden on a place already fragile with hunger. In spring, when her mage abilities swelled with the buds, she could gradually wake her hunger with delicate greens, and feast in summer. But not too much…

The intruder was so determined to stalwartly power his way through the virginal, knee-deep snow that he hadn't noticed her. "Are you looking for me?" she called. Only, her words rasped. She hadn't spoken in a long time.

He heard her, though, and stopped. And looked around.

"Here," she offered helpfully.

His gaze settled on her. For a moment she felt exposed, vulnerable despite the great disparity of power in her favor, but then he bowed his head again and trudged toward her. She moved to meet him. Her lightly booted feet crunched down only halfway into the dry, powdery snow, while her long woolen skirts floated on the surface, but she didn't mind the slight touch of frost that kissed her through her stockings She hoped that she didn't smell of sweat. She didn't bathe much in winter. Hopefully his nose was numb.

The man stopped a few feet away, so close she could see the individual frost crystals on his dark beard. Dark-skinned, dark-eyed, he looked smart, and strong. He blushed and lowered his gaze. Maybe it was because he found her attractive, but she doubted it. More likely he wasn't sure how to address a mage, especially one rumored to dislike intruders. Only, she didn't dislike them. She didn't like what they asked of her.

"Ms. Green," the man said. He had a nice voice. "My name is Brennen. There's a building our city has been attempting to make new," he said. "But there's a ghost. No one has been able to shift it. I've come a very long way, and I hope you'll follow me the very long way back to my home."

She wondered if anyone had died trying to shift the ghost. She hoped not.

She wondered if his home was her former home. She wondered if this was a ruse.

It was so long ago that all the bad things happened.

Wherever he took her it would be...not this. This aloneness. Which was fine, aloneness was fine, it was good because she could control her emotions better and therefore her magic better, but she did miss some things sometimes. "Will there be apples?" she asked.

He smiled, which made him very handsome. It was her turn to blush, though it also made her sad. She'd loved a handsome man once. "Yes," he said.

A brief breeze lifted his scent to her face. He was perfumed, which would have been nice if it wasn't so strong. She preferred the more gentle, warm scents of his skin underneath.

She wasn't sure she could live like a person again. She remembered being happy once. The price of that happiness was too high. "Then I'll come with you," she told him. Not to stay, though.

Never to stay again.

§

He'd hired a room for her on a cloud ship. It felt unbearably warm and tight inside. If she'd had money, she would have paid him back, because she couldn't stand to sleep there. She slept on the deck instead, braced up against the main mast, head tipped back so she could watch the clouds by day and the stars by night, the sky framed by sails not nearly as pristine as snow. She also spent some time at the rail and stared at the wintery landscape below as they flew higher than the tallest trees. The only time she used her room was when then made a stop in Long View.

Long View was where the mage Jular had convinced her that he loved her.

She'd fought by his side to protect Long View from a godling that wanted to be a king. All that blood, and afterward all the pain, had driven her toward Heavens Mountain as if she were snow in a storm. The wilderness was quiet, and peaceful. There, where resources were scarce and with no one to betray her, it was unlikely that she'd become like the godling they'd fought. If all went to plan, her powers would peak, and then age and begin to fail until finally she would fade into that place where magic resided beyond the living and the dead.

Her gut twinged with anxiety. What if Brennen was lying? Would his people try to make her kill a godling again? It was harder to trust each time she came back to do a thing for people, but ever since the break with Jular, they hadn't betrayed her.

So far.

The city Brennen took her to, Rose City, was at a confluence of two massive rivers. Bethmay sighed a bit at the carriage awaiting them at the sky pier. The carriage had gilding and glass all over it. She supposed it was time to acclimate herself to an interior life, but did it have to begin like this?

Once she sat on the red leather seat with Brennen across from her, and Brennen closed the most-glass door, her heart began to race. She forced herself to take deep, slow breaths through her nose. The perfume was even more concentrated, and the sunlight swelled the trapped air with moisture and heat. She'd bathed and washed her clothes on the ship, and the soap had been perfumed so she thought she'd be used to it by now. But she was not, and she sweated like an icicle in a greenhouse.

"Is everything all right?" Brennen asked.

"Mmm," she said non-committedly, and kept her gaze rooted outside the window. The horses began their work, pulling them across smooth brick toward the nearest bridge. The bridge had crystal lights, always shining even in the brilliance of this soft winter's day. There were so many it would be impossible to see the stars at night.

Though they were below the snow line, Brennen had dressed warmly. She opened a side window, desperate for relief, and breathed in the soothing chill.

"Would you like me to open my window as well?" Brennen asked.

She wanted to say yes. "It's time I get used to it." The cool breeze on her face helped.

"Not too used to it," Brennen told her with a smile. "There's no heat in the building yet, and they haven't put in all the windows. But it does have walls and a roof."

"Good." He probably thought that she approved of the walls and roof, but she was actually relieved that all the glazing wasn't in yet.

"Are you sure you're all right?" Brennen asked.

"I haven't been back to civilization in a while. I haven't even spoken with anyone since…" She had to think. Had it been two years already? These stretches of her being alone were getting longer. Maybe that was a good thing. She didn't know.

"Since when?" Brennen prompted.

"Since the last time someone asked me to kill one of my kind for them. I told them no." They had accepted that no graciously, but hadn't been gracious enough to not ask in the first place.

She'd learned later that Jular had died, but everyone had been too afraid to tell her how. That probably meant his magic had overtaken him, and he'd been killed.

"We won't ask you to kill anyone, mage or human," Brennen assured her.

"I will kill if I have to," she warned him, and watched the city lights sparkle like gems in the sunlight. "Just not for you."

§

While Bethmay listened and observed Brennen explaining about the building, Bethmay noticed he was observing her.

The builders had restored what they believed was the exact layout of the upper floor based on old descriptions. The main floor would become public space, with most of it left open as a large, marble-floored gallery. In a room to one side a bronze tree sculpture with storybook characters had been cleaned and polished, a memorial to honor the building's original use as a library in the days before magic burst across the world, triggering both a renaissance and countless catastrophes.

All around and on the upper floors, people mopped and hammered and painted the building back to life, restoring its beauty.

The trouble was below ground level. Bethmay steeled herself as they went down flight after broad flight of a stone staircase lit by crystal lights set in the walls near their feet. It wasn't awful, but the air felt very still here. Bethmay reminded herself that they weren't trying to trap her. Jular always used to remind her of that. It surprised her that it was his voice in her mind that helped soothe her now.

The stairs ended at a large room where several broad halls met. Brennen led her to the right.

This part of the building, Brennen explained, had been in use right up until the roof caved in. By then the whole rest of the building had been in a state of terrible disrepair. Just before they abandoned it, it had been used as a refuge for the mentally ill, and also a poor farm.

Though it was underground and near a river, the space was dry. Brennen's breath made mist in the hallway. Unlike the rest of the building, the walls and ceiling were roughly made, plastered, and washed with lime, probably repartitioning the original spaces that once existed here. Brennen noticed Bethmay looking up. "They had few resources, and the books that might have taught them to do better had been ruined or stolen. Still, it's not all that bad. I think that the fragile whiteness of the lime wash helped keep it from feeling oppressive, as well as it keeping it clean."

It felt oppressive to Bethmay, but she didn't say so.

Doorways leading to an alternating single rooms and suites. Signs of work—tools, buckets, mops—lay about, but the two of them were the only ones here.

"The single rooms were used for small families or groups of people who could get along," Brennen told her. "The suites were for extended families and larger groups. It was crowded."

Most of the doorways had new oak doors on them. The fresh stain on them gave the air a sharp, not-unpleasant tang of turpentine and fine oil. One doorway did not have a door. The doorway had some debris in front of it: a piece of shattered wood, some dust, a glove, a bit of broken stone.

"And there's the room with the ghost," Brennen said, gesturing to the doorway with the debris. "No one has even managed to get a name. I've been researching who might have lived in this room, but I've had no luck."

"Why the mess by the door?" Bethmay asked, drawn to step carefully closer. She couldn't sense anything yet, but that wasn't unusual.

"The ghost piles it there."

Building a wall, Jular said in her mind. "All right. I'll get to work."

"Do you need anything?"

To be done with this. "No. I get by with very little." But that was a reflexive answer, born from old hurts and betrayals. "I'd like to have an apple, but mostly I need privacy and quiet."

"We'll gladly give you whatever you need to make this happen as quickly and safely as possible," Brennen assured her.

"So the ghost is violent." She wasn't surprised.

"When provoked, yes. And we haven't figured out what provokes it, yet."

"The door?" Bethmay wondered aloud. "Maybe it doesn't want one."

Brennen let out a sigh. "We're not sure, actually. We know little about it."

Bethmay stepped closer. Now she felt it: a prickling across her skin, a tension in her gut, the sense that something had recoiled from her like a spider drawing its legs deep into the crack it had made its home. She sat down, braced her back against the wall, and began to relax. She started with the expression on her face, allowing the muscles to soften, her eyes to half-close, her breaths moving smoothly through her nose and out through barely-parted lips. Her soul stretched its wings and the air around her cooled. She sighed with relief and the crystal lights in the hall dimmed.

Brennen remained, silently standing guard. His quiet presence was just what she needed to let down her guard enough to use her magic.

§

Bethmay sank into the stones, or so it felt. She had no idea what someone watching might see, and the deeper she went down, the less she cared. This place was cool and calm, but it was also a sad place, a gray place of dust, bare bones and dirty, lost toys.

A whisper of something tugged at her. She was tempted to speak aloud, but whatever had spoken probably wouldn't hear her. She sensed menace there, but mostly searching, an echo to her own search, but foreign to her.

She sank deeper, toward the sound, but she wasn't sure where to find it. The deeper she went, the darker things were. But there were shapes now, shapes other than the bleak coolness of that almost-graveyard within the stones.

Within her mind a void opened. She believed it was a shadowy echo of the room with the debris in front of it, but the debris wasn't there. The room had four cots in it, with barely any room to get between them. Each cot was surrounded by blankets hung from ropes strung across the ceiling. They'd hung clothes from the ropes as well. It was revolting, these close quarters, the tightness in the room. She started to feel lost in it, lost among the blankets and clothes. Where was the door? Where was the door, the door, the door…

Bethmay escaped with a gasp back into the hallway. She was sitting where she'd been before. With effort she controlled her breathing and kept her magic in tight control.

"Are you all right?" Brennen asked.

"Yes." She didn't easily feel cold, but now a chill ached in her hands and feet. She stood up and blew into her hands, gazing into the empty, windowless room. Had what she'd seen been part of the troublesome ghost, or some strong memory that belonged to the room? She approached the door with respect. If it was a ghost, it had the power to hurt her, or even kill her. If it was just a strong memory, she might get caught up in it enough to hurt herself, but the threat was much less.

Best to assume the ghost was awake for now.

Words were seldom what someone who was lost and alone wanted to hear. Instead, she hummed a few notes from Ombly Fair, a song nearly everyone who spoke Athan knew.

Something tugged at her mind, like seeing a face she recognized in a crowd, but instead it was the empty room that caught her attention. As if she'd looked into a warped, dirty mirror, the insubstantial thing in the room began to resolve into something she recognized within herself.

Loneliness.

That meant it was human once, and that meant that the ghost was here now.

She slowly approached the threshold, still humming softly. She watched, *sensed* that reflection as best she could, searching for signs of a change of expression. It wasn't easy to do while paying attention to the physical world. She couldn't afford to trip and fall, or stumble into a wall, but neither could she afford to take much more than a sliver of her full attention away from the room.

The reflection in her mind grew more distinct. She could see the cots, the laundry hung on ropes strung as close to the ceiling as possible, the lime wash white and fresh on the walls, obscuring the gray grime that had accumulated over time. And there was a shadow, a translucent darkness with hints of eyes and a darker slash for a mouth. So faint, like smoke that could be tasted but barely tinged the air…

The hairs on her arms stood up. She set her hand on the wall beside the doorway, still humming. The ghost didn't move, but the energy in the room coiled up tight. Bethmay froze and stopped humming. Her breath frosted in the air in the doorway. She sucked it back inside herself and held her breath. Loneliness seeped inside her. It stared into her and she stared back and it felt like she'd become an autumn leaf that detached from the tree and drifted slowly toward the ground, toward the ghost that needed…

The shadow uncoiled and drifted toward her, and her thoughts uncoiled and touched the ghost. That first contact hollowed her out. Her lips parted and her breath failed. Her heart clenched and then swelled in her chest, desperate to beat but she was trapped in the doorway.

Not her.

Not her!

Fiery pain split across her cheek and darkness filled her sight. Her back and head cracked against stone. She choked, her gaze now locked on the top of the doorway and the lime ceiling. The ghost swept over her like a blanket of cobwebs. A hand of smoke poured into her gaping mouth and filled the inside of her throat—

Brennen grabbed her and dragged her down the hall. His mouth pressed over hers and his breath stopped hard in her throat. He listened at her chest and then he loomed over her, arms locked straight, hands over her ribs. He thrust down hard, crushing her ribs, over and over, squeezing her heart, her lungs. Everything was so tight inside her she thought she would burst open or her guts would be forced out of her mouth—

Her heart clenched and the pain made her want to scream. She couldn't. Her heart clenched again, firing the mage power within her. It built up inside her until the pressure was almost unbearable. She struggled to control it and shape it while Brennen once again covered her mouth with his and tried to breathe for her. His breath broke through her throat just as the power within her exploded outward. She made it into a force that threw him back as she vomited the ghost's grip out from inside her.

Bethmay gasped and stood, grabbing for the ghost with her mage energy. The ghost slipped away. She tore at it's tattered edges, chasing it back to the door. She almost had it again—

Brennen grabbed her and yanked her out of the room.

The ghost had vanished. She sagged within Brennen's arms in the hall, gasping for air, her heart thundering in her ears and pounding in her chest and throat. For long moments she couldn't speak. Anger and frustration built up while she gathered breath after breath. She realized then that it was good she couldn't speak. If she'd unleashed that anger now, the unshaped mage energy could hurt or even kill Brennen.

Brennen had saved her life.

"Thank you," she managed to say without releasing a dangerous amount of mage energy. She tamped down on her frustration, balling it up in her gut and her mind while it thrashed and demanded to be known. If she'd been entirely human it would have done no harm to express herself, but her emotions were laced with her inherited mage power and she didn't dare unleash them. "Though next time, trust that if I'm on my feet and my eyes are glowing, I'm fine." Her breath settled quickly but her heart was still pounding.

"What happened?"

It wasn't easy to put into words. "I formed a connection. He was fine until he realized I wasn't who he thought I was. Then he attacked. I might have survived on my own, but it could have gone either way. Thank you for reviving me." She needed Brennen to know that he hadn't done anything wrong, though he had gotten in her way. "Unfortunately by the time you got my heart going again I was too desperate for air to keep hold of the ghost. In truth, he had a hold on me too." Her heart eased in its frantic rhythm. "I had to force him out to breathe. And then I chased after him and I almost caught him, but you pulled me back and I lost him."

"I was afraid that if you went in that room the ghost would kill you."

"It would have been a fight," she assured him. "I would have won, though."

Brennen averted his gaze. Until he did, she hadn't noticed how close he stood, and how completely his attention and life energy had been focused on her. It warmed her, and made her feel like…

…a person.

"I didn't know," he said softly.

He had to find the connection he now had to her uncomfortable, even painful. She didn't want to give up the warmth, but she had to for his sake. She used her energy to gently slip his energy off of her like he was a blanket. It exposed her to the cold in the air, in the stones, and emptied her heart of human warmth.

She'd forgotten how good real warmth felt. She could imagine basking in his presence like basking in the summer sun, could imagine smiling.

But she could also imagine him rejecting her, like Jular. It was one thing to entwine magical energies. Energy had no personality, no wants or needs. It glowed like a fire and shared its warmth without thought or expectation. It was entirely different to entwine lives, to care. With friendship and love came the inevitable battles. Like two trees growing together, branches intermingled, things were good until the soil grew too poor, until they began to choke each other. And even when they survived and thrived, if one fell it left the other bare of branches on one side, forever lopsided.

Lopsided like she'd been when Jular ended it with her.

She wondered if he felt her absence, or if he'd grown on without her, maybe with someone else. It was more likely that he'd never grown with her at all, though. She hadn't been a tree to him. She'd been more like a vine he'd invited to twine around him, and when he was done with her, he pried her off and she collapsed without him.

"I'm sorry," Brennen said.

The regret in his voice stabbed her. "You did nothing wrong." She needed him to know that. "You saved my life." And then she thought of what she'd done. "Did I hurt you?"

"No," he said, but he put a hand to his back. "Is it always like this when you shift ghosts?"

The warmth of his concern started to wrap around her again. She stepped away and turned her back to him. "No. The ghost's energy and mine are similar. He's missing the tree that used to grow alongside him." She realized that would make no sense to Brennen, but that didn't matter. "When he realized that I wasn't who he needed, he reacted badly." It wasn't until she spoke the words that she thought of the perfect way to shift the ghost. But it was horrific. It was what Jular had done to her. "I need to rest. In the morning, I'll try again."

"I've always known it's dangerous work, but I'd never witnessed… I don't know that you should try again. Maybe we should just board up the room."

"You would leave the ghost in misery, and there's no certainty that he wouldn't change. He might leave the room and attack someone. He might grow in strength and consume the building room by room with death energy. He needs to go." She wondered if Jular had been as certain about shifting her out of his life, and the lives of the people of High Barrow.

It made no difference now. Now, she had a ghost to shift so that life could take back this place. "We could surrender to death," she told Brennen. "Leave places like this to ghosts. But in time the whole world would stagnate and become dead. The dead have other places. This world belongs to the living. The living need to hold it against death." And magic, she thought. "Though death will always have a presence here, of course." Like magic would always have a presence.

The irony twisted her gut. She'd been existing in a kind of living death and now she was lecturing someone who was far more alive than she about value of life. "I'd like to go to my room now, please."

He offered his arm but she didn't accept. He wouldn't have offered it if he knew what she was about to do.

§

She began humming Ombly Fair, and when she had the ghost's attention again she sent gentle, apologetic energy to him. That was all. And then she left. The next day she returned and watched the ghost between bouts of reading a book while eating apples. She let the pleasure from eating apples and reading bleed into the room. And then she started reading short passages to him.

She filled those empty places where the branches of his life hadn't grown, because his wife and child had filled those spaces. And over days, weeks, she invited him to twine around her existence.

Bethmay knew what to do because Jular had taught her. She let little things that the ghost did displease her, and then quickly forgave him. She skipped days, so that he would feel sad when she didn't arrive at the anticipated time. She sometimes surprised him by arriving early, and often stayed late, then would arrive late and leave early the next day. She kept him off balance until he began to twine around her energy, eager to please her. He forgot his wife and child. He started seeing the room for what it was: barren and dead. He grew to long for more, even as his longing for her grew.

And in her mind he grew as well into a large man with a soft voice and gentle eyes. He had a temper. She had to often remind herself of it. He was overly possessive, and clinging. And yet, he was so sweet.

She arrived on the morning she'd decided to take him at her usual hour. He sensed right away something was off with her. She didn't try to hide it. She drew him in with half-truths about how she'd had such hopes that he would be more than he is, but how again and again she'd find him in the same place doing the same things over and over. She told him that she couldn't be with him in this place, and that she saw no future for him. She told him that although she loved him, which was the same awful lie that Jular had told her, she couldn't be with him as long as he stayed in that room.

And of course he swore he would change, and he ventured to the doorway. All he needed was more time and encouragement. All he needed was a chance and he promised he would follow her wherever she wanted to go.

She used the momentum of his movement toward her, seizing him with her mage gift fueled by the twisting, agonizing emotions that screamed that she was a monster for betraying him. He tried to slip free but she threw everything she had into the barrier between life and death, using the ghost like a hammer. The air warped and darkness opened a hungry mouth, swallowing the ghost. It sucked at her too, at the revulsion she felt toward herself, the despair, the loneliness, the memories of Jular's betrayal and her lost happiness—

Strong arms grabbed her and threw her into a wall. The sharp pain of soft flesh slamming into cold, hard stone woke her to the danger she posed to Brennen while her emotions ran wild. She balled up her mage power and feelings into a hard knot inside her.

The mouth closed.

She was alone with Brennen.

The doorway nearby revealed an empty room, gaping and hollow in its profound emptiness.

She'd never know if she destroyed the ghost, or if she'd successfully cast him into death. With so many forces tearing at him at once, there might not have been enough left of him on the other side to survive.

She didn't want to know. She wanted to go back to the wilderness and pretend that she did the right thing. She had to believe that she would always help people and protect the living. And the world needed protection, from the lingering dead but also from people so infected by magic that it twisted them into tyrants and monsters.

"I have to go," she told Brennen, sickened by what she'd done.

Brennen let her go. It wasn't until he released her that she realized she was trembling.

"I'm sorry," he said.

He was always apologizing for doing the right thing. "You saved my life again."

Brennen nodded, but it wasn't in the way of someone agreeing. His eyes were gazing away, lost among thoughts he'd likely never speak aloud to her. But then his gaze returned to her. "You should stay."

He was wrong. "It's dangerous. I don't want…" She didn't want to risk the chance that she might lose control of her powers or worse, her mind. Then someone like Jular would have to come and kill her, to save people and perhaps the world from a godling. She wondered briefly whether she'd want to reign, or just feast to feed a never-ending hunger. Or maybe she'd want to bring more and more magic into the world until the world was filled with wonders. It would be so beautiful, but of course the people and animals would fall prey to things that they couldn't defend themselves against. The realm of magic would consume this fragile, lovely world she'd been born into. It would be so wrong…

"You don't want what?" Brennen asked.

She opened her mouth to explain, but the words she expected didn't emerge. "To be alone."

"You're alone out there in the wilderness."

She was. "But there, it's my choice. There's no hope of friendship out there. But that's better than to be here and be treated like a monster.

Because I am a monster." That confession wrecked her. It filled her up with the past, with Jular, with lost joy and present loneliness. It wasn't safe to be here. It wasn't safe for Brennen. She couldn't even tell him that for fear of hurting him.

Bethmay hurried down the hall, up the stairs, out to the night where the crystal lights bleached the stars nearly to nothingness. She shaped the magic boiling up within her, grew wings, and flew home.

§

Bethmay hunted for the source of smoke that wafted in a large cloud through the shadowy understory of tall fir trees. And then she saw Brennen. She'd expected hunters and had planned on letting them know that she wouldn't allow them to take any large game north of the stream that she fished on. She thought about turning back, thought about hiding, but left on his own he would travel onward to the meeting point. She might as well greet him here and find out what he needed.

He'd saved her life. She couldn't refuse him.

He was dressed in layers like he had been the last time, but lighter layers. Even with the fire, it had to feel chilly to them in the deep shade. And, if she had to be honest, she had to admit she felt a little chilled too.

Brennen had done that to her, with his quiet words and how he knew when she was in danger, even when she couldn't speak. She wondered if he intuitively knew how much more keenly she felt the aloneness now. It was no longer fine, this aloneness. She was actually lonely. She feared she wouldn't be able to say no if he asked her to come stay with him in the city. She needed to say no, though. Her emotions were already growing hotter, wilder with every step she took closer to him.

"Are you looking for me?" she called. Her voice didn't catch, but it sounded uncertain. At least she'd been using it. She'd been humming and singing more lately. She didn't know what that meant. Probably nothing good.

He stood as she crossed the last distance to their camp. She stayed opposite the fire from him. The smoke drifted lazily at a low angle to the ground, scented sweetly of cedar. Brennen blushed. It made him more handsome, which made her sad, but also thrilled her.

This wasn't love. But it was the start of a friendship, and a possibility of love. That made him dangerous to her, and also everything short of irresistible.

Brennen's gaze remained softly on Bethmay's face.

She started to tell him that she wouldn't kill for him, but this time it wasn't true. This time, she would. More, this time she was ready. She felt poised on the verge of becoming a godling. If he knew this, and she suspected that he knew, she would take her own life if he asked her to, and travel to the realm of magic where she would finally belong. Her breaths shortened and her heart quickened and her hands went cold and felt numb. Her lips tingled. She could do it, but she was afraid. The fear made every sense clamor for attention. It felt as if her body had become a busy marketplace with countless vendors calling out their wares and people jostling and laughing and shouting…

She would do it not because she loved him, but because she trusted him more than she trusted herself now, and because it was time. Even mages couldn't live forever. She'd planned on growing old and fading away. But her encounter with the ghost, and with Brennen, had unearthed something that she couldn't bury again.

"Ms. Green," Brennen said.

She nodded. She didn't dare speak until her heart steadied, assuming it ever would again.

"May I stay here with you?" he asked.

She stepped back, shocked.

Brennen blushed again, deepening his already dark skin, but he didn't look away. "I don't know what I feel," he said. "But I'd like to learn, if I may. I know I might die out here. But that would be better than what I've been through these past months."

She wanted to ask him what he'd been through. She didn't understand. But she couldn't speak.

"Nothing feels as real as those moments when you shifted the ghost," he said. "The city, the building, the day to day work has no meaning anymore. I want…I want to see more, to experience more, to learn more of all the worlds. Not just ours. You know I'm not afraid. I want to help you protect life, if I can. If I may."

The warmth of his caring eased the chill in the shadows.

Bethmay took several deep breaths before her heart steadied enough to speak. But with every word her heart lifted with pain and joy and gut-wrenching fear. Fear for him, fear for her future, raw fear that roamed aimlessly and snapped and snarled at what she was about to do. But she said the words anyway. "You. May."

"Thank you."

The thanks surprised Bethmay.

"It will be dangerous," she warned.

"I'll be all right," he assured her, still gazing at her with warmth.

That was wrong. "You might not be," Bethmay warned, and the words carried power that filled the air with pressure and dampened the fire. "I'm…not well."

"I'll help, if I can," he said again. "If I may."

Her heart calmed, and the fire crackled with fresh vigor. She smiled for the first time in a long time. She was no longer alone. He was right. They would both be all right. "You may," she said.

Suzanne Hagelin has lived as varied and interesting a life as she could manage—growing up in Mexico City, living in the Middle East, traveling and exploring the world, learning languages, working in IT, family, exchange students, teaching, volunteering, and translating. She settled in the Seattle area where she runs an indie publishing company, Varida Press, with a small group of authors, and teaches language on the side. Her books include the sci-fi *Body Suit* and contemporary fiction *The Artist*.

DREAM SEQUENCE

Suzanne Hagelin

A t first there was a smell, a sickly-sweet odor in an aromatic fog, filling Weylah with unease bordering on alarm. It was followed by sharp pain in the back of her skull, as if a huge needle had punctured it. Then the pain vanished, and she could see a cloud, bluish with feathered streaks of red, and murky lights glimmering through. After a moment, the mist and the scent dispersed, but the taste of danger remained, leaving her mouth dry.

"Hold the flask on the back of your hand," Weylah heard. They were the first words she was aware of, almost like a dream. She glanced down at her hand where it lay on an armrest and saw a glass of sorts, half full of water, balancing on the back of her hand.

"Like this?" she asked as she took in more of her surroundings. A chair. That made sense. Armrests were usually attached to chairs. And they often looked just like this one when they were in an office or a clinic of some sort.

"That will be fine," someone said. She became aware of the clinic. All the normal aspects were there; a waiting area with children playing with some toys in the corner, and a reception desk with a non-descript person answering questions.

Was this right? Would she have someone instructing her in the lobby instead of an examination room? The scene twisted and began to morph.

Wait. This wasn't the lobby. That was a wall over there, not the play area.

She looked back down at her hand. The glass was pink, and the water bubbly. *Am I thirsty?* she wondered. Sometimes she dreamed of water when…was this a dream?

Weylah jerked her head around looking for the source of the words she'd been listening to. She was alone in the room. The motion made the flask wobble and splash water onto her fingers. Her brief concern was swept away by the conviction that it didn't matter. Yanking her hand out, she grabbed the glass without spilling a drop. *Ha!* she thought, bringing it to her lips. Cold, fresh water.

81

She couldn't taste it.

She set the glass down and rose to her feet. Was that a commotion outside? Or maybe in the lobby? A low rumbling sound and faint voices carried toward her from the distance, little whines in the wind.

With one step she reached the door and pulled it open.

The scene that met her eyes was chaotic, beyond her ability to grasp. She stared around in a stupor, taking it all in, struggling to make sense of it. It was as if gravity didn't make sense anymore, and up and down wouldn't stay in place. Things were whirling around and slamming into buildings or cars or whatever those moving objects were. Not a tornado. That would have some sense of motion she could interpret, fitting into a spinning, whipping pattern. This was all mixed up.

She took a step out into the wild and found her foot landing on solid ground that stayed where it should. "What is going on?" she yelled into the wind, the words were swallowed by the noise.

She took a few more steps and realized she could walk, and the visual distortion wasn't a true interpretation of what surrounded her. There were wind and noise, but as she walked, she could make out a bit of sidewalk under her feet, and here and there, people, sitting or standing motionless staring up at the mess.

"What is all this?" she asked a kid who crouched with his arms in a semicircle.

"Quiet!" he hissed at her. "I'm trying to get it to trust me. Back away and go around behind me!" There was nothing she could see nearby but she imagined an animal, maybe injured. He was trying to coax it into his embrace so he could take care of it. For a moment she was tempted to squat next to him and help. After all, she was pretty good with animals.

No, she shook her head. The roar of the storm blasted her again. There was nothing there and she didn't intend to take that tangent. This was clearly a dream and she wanted to know what it all meant.

The turbulence crystalized into a city street with a mighty storm beating at the buildings and buffeting the people, like herself, who were foolish enough to be out in it. The whole purpose of the windblasts seemed to be to force her inside. Anywhere.

She stubbornly stayed outdoors, shivering in the cold, getting drenched by the rain. Had it been raining at first? She didn't know.

Then the flashes began, like lightning but all wrong. It didn't arc from land to sky or from sky to land. They sliced sideways, at angles, sometimes in single thread-like beams, sometimes in scattered explosions. Like fireworks.

Weylah stopped walking and stared. The people she had been passing were being vaporized, one by one. The wave of death rolled up the street, taking down buildings as it neared her, but no one noticed except for her. Everywhere she looked, people were busy, preoccupied with little things that didn't matter, and the ripple of destruction took them without warning.

She was looking right at it, her mouth wide open, shrieking into the wind, but she was unable to hear anything besides the roar it made, and never saw the flash when it pierced her.

It all faded.

Weylah opened her eyes and found herself in the room again, sitting in the chair. Only this time, there was no flask on her hand. An attendant sat across from her, eyes on a pad where he tapped and clicked, making notes.

A clock was ticking nearby. *That means time is moving forward*, she thought.

She looked at the attendant, waiting for him to lift his eyes so she could speak. He never did. She spoke anyway.

"Excuse me," she said, using her polite manner. "Can I ask what I'm waiting for?"

The man glanced up at her, a distinctly smug look on his face, but said nothing. He went back to his notes.

"Am I waiting on results? I'm not sure what…"

"The test is over," he said, gesturing toward a passageway on her right that led to a sunny glass door.

She looked down the hall with the strong impression that it led to waking up. Then turned to her left to look at the door she had gone out earlier in the dream.

The attendant ignored her.

Normally, she would prefer to wake up, especially in this kind of dream, but something made her hesitate. Nightmares bring terror—but she wasn't afraid, just more alert, aware of both realms while sleeping. And there was an underlying tension that triggered something deeper than dream fear.

She jumped to her feet and ran toward the door to her left.

"Not that way," a voice behind her called.

She ignored it and pulled open the door to the outside.

The streets she had seen before awaited her and a storm was kicking up. It began moaning and slamming loose doors, knocking things over, whipping trash and debris around. It was almost as if the dream had started over and she was stepping into it earlier than she had the first time.

She made her way down the sidewalk, passing people occupied with various mindless pursuits like watching a butterfly, playing with a yo-yo, kicking a can, scratching patterns in the dirt, trying to catch a skittish cat.

"Hey!" she found herself saying as she turned to look at the kid she had noticed the first time. "What happened to it?" Inside she was wondering, *did her mind fill in the cat or was it easier to see because the storm hadn't blown out of control yet?*

"I don't know," he said. "She ran out the door and she's never done that before. She's really scared…" He circled his arms and squatted, cornering the cat. It wavered between looking at him fondly and staring over his shoulder. Then its hair rose on end and its tail puffed as the noise of the tempest began to increase. The sidewalk underneath them swayed and dipped, like the entire city was inside a rocking cradle.

"Come on," Weylah patted the boy's arm. "Let her go. We've got to run before the full brunt of the storm hits."

He looked up at her in confusion. "The what?" he said, and his eyes bulged, as if he hadn't noticed the noise till that moment. "What's happening?" The cat ran past him into the distance.

"Come on!" she yelled and they both ran the same direction.

The wave of destruction, crashing and exploding behind them, poured down the streets in their wake. Most of the people they passed seemed to be unaware of it. Weylah slapped at their arms or pushed them as she ran past, calling them, but unable to slow down to try to wake them up.

There was no time.

"Come on! Come on!" the kid screamed, kicking into high gear and tearing down the road faster than her. The skies overhead were getting darker, billowing with solid clouds of storm. Or was it like ash from a volcano?

The roar grew louder till it shook her body as it vibrated through her. She should have been terrified, but wasn't. There was still that strong sense of *something else*.

She never saw the end. She just stopped vibrating and opened her eyes again in the clinic chair. The attendant was sitting in the same place, still tapping the pad. She stared at him for a moment, knowing he was aware of her, waiting for him to say something, or just look up. He didn't. But she knew he wasn't feeling quite as smug as he had the first time.

This is my dream, she considered, in my head.

He paused, finger poised over the pad, listening. Aware.

Somewhere in my brain, I know what he's typing.

The attendant's eyes lifted to hers and glanced away. He definitely wasn't looking as smug as he had before.

She jumped to her feet and ran for the door to the left again. This was a puzzle and she was going to figure it out.

"Wait!" a voice called, "Well done! You've passed the test!"

Outside, the buildings, sidewalks, roads, and people were all the same as before, but not everyone was doing the same thing as before. Some of them had shifted. They must be on a different loop, if that was the right word, and her story was the only one repeating. The woman with the butterfly had coaxed it onto her finger. The man with the yo-yo had stopped swinging it around and was studying the pattern etched in its side. The old guy kicking the can had disappeared.

The kid who had tried to catch the cat was watching her as she approached. As if he had been waiting for her.

"You!" he said.

"Where's your cat?" she countered, glancing over her shoulder to see if the wave had started.

"She got away last time," he said, backing up as if he wanted her to run with him again.

"Did the wave get you?" she asked as she started jogging next to him. They passed several of the same people as before.

"Yeah. I don't know."

A woman scrolling on her phone raised her eyebrows in recognition as they went by. "Aren't you the one who pushed me last time?" she asked Weylah, "Why did you do that?"

The dream was looping but the people weren't.

That was important.

"We've got to get away from the storm," the kid answered before she could.

They began collecting people as they ran. There were at least twelve as the storm began raging and overtaking them. At the last second before it vaporized them, she turned around to look into it, wanting to see what it was, what lay behind the power.

Time slowed. Her body twisted in slow motion and her eyes focused on the broiling storm cloud, the shock wave. She planted her feet and burrowed into it with her mind as well as her gaze. And she saw something behind the destruction.

A being. Multiple beings, running along with lasers in their hands, gunning down everything in their path. They had rectangular torsos with faces in the middle and they seemed like they were having fun.

"NO!" she yelled at them, unable to hear the sound from her own lips.

One of them almost ran into her and paused as if startled.

She closed her eyes. The crash. The flash. The quiet. The room.

There was the attendant again and he wasn't tapping notes this time.

She was back in the chair. She focused on the pad in his hands and projected her understanding toward it. *All is going well*, it said at the top. *Apathy is an easily spread substance. Thoroughly effective at rendering them helpless.*

Something in her knew that the words hadn't been in English—and she had supplied the translation.

A minor difficulty...followed after a break in the notes, subject behaving erratically. No need for concern...

Weylah was pretty sure she was the 'subject' and 'apathy' was the cloud over the minds of the people in her dream.

"Who are you?" she asked with less force than she had meant to project, feeling a little weary from the running around. *I should sit here for a moment to recover*, she thought.

The attendant's eyes didn't lift up to look at her, but he was *intensely* aware of her. Why would she dream of him? What did he mean in her mind?

She rose to her feet calmly this time, took a step and snatched the pad out of his hands. It was blank. "It is not blank," she said. Words began to form on the surface in not quite legible shapes and flourishes that resembled letters but meant nothing.

"I can read it," she said, and she recognized the meaning she had already discerned even though the lines on the screen remained unintelligible. Handing the pad back to him, she turned and walked toward the door on the left again. He didn't try to stop her.

Outside, the kid was waiting for her. He must have figured out which door was hers which struck her as being very cool. "What are we going to do?" he asked. "We can't just keep running."

She looked at him carefully, studying his face, wanting to remember it when she awoke—because he *was* a real person, not just the product of a dreaming mind. She was sure of it.

"What's your name?" she asked.

"Digo. You?"

"Weylah...or Wey..." She wasn't sure why she added the nickname of her childhood.

"Oh," he said.

"Did you look at them?" She faced the direction the storm always came from.

"I was going to...when you turned around," he answered, his eyes widening as he stood beside her, facing the same way. "But all I saw was the lightning strike and you puffed into a swirl of smoke..." He gestured with his hands, pantomiming the explosion. "Then I was gone again."

86

"Where do you wake up after that?"

"My room…I'm supposed to be straightening it but the cat…" he scratched his head and scrunched his nose as if he had to add pressure to his skull in order to figure it out.

"Look out!" Weylah cried out. The tossing clouds and torrents of wind were upon them. "There! There!" she added in a screech that barely carried over the noise.

"I see!" he yelled back in his boyish voice.

The beings were running toward them, waving triangular loops of glowing metal, shooting out bolts of blue and white from the points, sometimes one, sometimes all three as it rotated in their grasp. Their faces gaped with triangular mouths and no teeth.

One ran up to the boy and another ran up to Weylah. Again, time slowed down. She was sure it was the same being as before, grinning, stretching its triangle till it filled the rectangular body with a black maw. The first time, it had been startled by her but now it chose her. Long fibrous strands hung from the top of its rectangular body like fringe. They were cords that turned their tips to look at her.

Eyes, she thought, hundreds of light receptacles scanning her.

Digo was backing away, one step at a time, just out of reach of the being's arm. It wasn't shooting at him. The one in front of her wasn't shooting either. It had stopped at the edge of her personal space and was twirling the laser gun on a spindly limb of some kind.

There was something repulsive about it and it made her angry. She shouted words at it, not sure what they were, challenging it. And as she continued voicing her defiance, she shoved her fist out in front of her, almost brushing its waving cords. The being shrunk back, the cords trembled—and she stepped toward it.

One punch, with no power in it. The kind that feels like you hardly moved because part of your brain knows you're sleeping, and the arm isn't moving. But the rage she felt was real. Her fist pushed up to it and sank into its gaping mouth, brushing against a cloudy fuzz that expanded like a bubble. The being exploded into chalky dust with streaks of several bright colors, pink, green, blue, like carnival ribbons. Like finger-paint colors.

In that one spot, the storm ceased, and time sped up again.

She whirled around, looking for Digo. He was staring at her in astonishment, the word "What?" half formed in his mouth when the being pursuing him blasted him.

Then Weylah was vaporized as well, struck from behind by another being.

She opened her eyes.

The attendant was sitting very still, holding onto the pad tightly with both hands, staring at it.

Invasion Tactics, the header read.

He couldn't just hang out in her dream without giving her access to those notes. He should've thought of that. The attendant closed his eyes. "You may depart," he said, and for the first time she noticed that his lips didn't move when he spoke.

Desensitization is very effective…proceeding according to plan…

"What are you doing to us?" she glowered at him.

Then the gist of the whole document suddenly pierced her understanding and she knew that this was not just a dream of an experiment with imaginary creatures.

She jumped to her feet.

How would a race of aliens test the possibility of invasion? What if they were approaching humans in dreams to see how they would handle an attack?

"Wait right there!" she commanded the attendant and ran to the door on the left as fast as she could, *knowing* he was stranded in her mind until she let him go.

Digo was holding a bat. "There's no way they're getting me this time," he yelled. "Here!" He tossed her a stick about three feet long.

"Quick!" Weylah called out as she caught it. "Let's round up as many people as we can before they get here." With that they started down the street, slapping, knocking, shoving people to get their attention. Some of them were already awake and aware of them.

"No, don't run!" they were crying. "Fight! We can do it!"

The aliens had created a scenario where people met their end in a puff of vapor, because it fit their own experience of extinction. *This* was what death looked like for them.

The rumbling started and the wind kicked up.

"Come on!" Weylah and Digo yelled to each other as they sprinted into the wind swinging their weapons.

Clouds of color burst in their wake as they barreled into the crowd of creatures. The storm dispelled in bubbles of quiet as the dust of each one settled to the ground. All around them people were fighting, and the noise of the battle spread down streets and blocks and across the neighborhood till the clouds were gone and a mighty cheer burst from the throats of the victors.

Sunshine began to brighten around them.

"No!" Weylah cried out with all her might. "Not yet!! Don't wake up! We're not done!" But all around her, people were vanishing and waking up from the dream.

"Digo!" she called, searching all around. But he was gone, too.

The light was encroaching on her mind, but she turned her back to it. *Not yet.* She wasn't about to leave that attendant lurking in her dream state. Where was the door she had come out of? She wandered down the chalk-covered road in the direction that felt right and soon found it.

She stepped back into the waiting room where the attendant waited, riveted to the spot where she had left him.

Weylah sat down across from him resting the stick on her knees. He stared down at his pad but was observing her keenly.

How many of them had come testing people in their dreams before this night? Was this the first time or was she just one peon in a batch, in a stream of batches of dreaming people?

Humans around the world were falling asleep as the planet turned and their homes entered the dark side of the world. Like a wave. They were accustomed to letting their minds ramble or stress or venture into unknown realms. Would they find a storm threatening?

She stared at the attendant. "How many?"

Many, she sensed his thought. He couldn't hide it from her. He had exposed himself when he entered her dream.

"How long?"

The answer was simultaneously past and future. She saw the Earth cycling in orbit halfway around the sun, turning on its axis. Half a year. *A few more planet rotations…*a few more days to go.

"Until what?" she insisted though her voice sounded calm—and she *knew* what.

Until we move in. He turned his eyes toward her as if he were unable to stop himself, as if he had more than two eyes. His hair seemed pulled toward her, and he was vibrating.

Somewhere, a mass of rectangular brutes was stretching and warming up. Laughing, practicing their target shooting, getting ready for the day that would soon come. This wasn't the first species they had conditioned not to resist. It had been a successful tactic a number of times.

"Why?"

The attendant's face was looking smug again. Its eyes were glowing a little and its head grew more horizontally oblong than before, though still humanoid. The illusion it had kept for her was fading. She saw another image in its mind, not rectangular like the parody of an alien they had decided to portray in the storm, but an aged, desiccated, barely moving lump of a body. Their real bodies, wherever they were out there, had been lovely once long ago. Now, they were nothing but chalk held together by thought, hardly moving, breathing husks at the end of their usefulness... soon to be vacated.

"Will you swipe your stick at me?" it asked as its mouth triangulated and shaped words laced with humor.

She could. He would turn into a puff of chalky dust and her dream would end. She would wake up and enter the real world where all this would seem distant and foolish. They would move on to the next batch and start again.

"I could," she replied, leaning forward. He shrunk back a bit, but the arrogance never left him.

Sometimes invasions were drawn out, bloody affairs.

Sometimes they were quick and unexpected.

Weylah didn't believe this was just a dream. From the beginning, the being had tried to get her to go out the door on the right and wake up. And each time she ran out the left door, they began the experiment again. If this was a precursor to an invasion, what were they afraid of? Why didn't they just overpower or imprison her?

"If you do not leave the dream, you will die here," it said, its corded fringe waving in the air, looking at her.

Sometimes invasions were high risk.

And sometimes...they backfired.

Weylah rose slowly to her feet, gripping the stick tightly in her hands. The being's face flicked back to a human shape again with alarm etched in its features. It sensed her intent and began screeching.

"Where is the door *you* came through?" She set her lips in a grim line. The link the attendant had made to access her mind—the one he didn't want her to notice—was open into *his* mind.

"Abort! Abort!" it began screaming, wheeling its limbs in a chaotic frenzy.

Then she saw the third door, straight behind him. Three strides took her there and she pulled it open with enough force to rip it off the hinges. The tempest raged out there in violent tosses of night-colored storm clouds and a wispy funnel shaped light snapped around in the center.

"You'll never survive!!" the alien was wailing as a sucking wind pulled it out the opening.

"Neither will you," she said as she gritted her teeth and stepped through after it.

Lawrence W. Powers, writing fiction as L. Wade Powers, has published previously in the NIWA anthologies. He is the author of two novels, *The Home* (2017) and *The Party House* (2019) and a short story collection, *Falling in Live and Other Misadventures* (2019). His author website is www.lwadepowers.com. He is currently writing a historical novel about Francis Drake on the Oregon coast in 1579 and the men left behind in New Albion. Larry is a retired university professor living on the dry side of Oregon.

THRESHOLD

L. Wade Powers

She had been there twice and beyond it once. It changed her. Not just frightened her, like a bad dream or an ominous warning. It possessed and manipulated her and by doing so, transformed my Marie into someone else. Physically, she looked much the same, an innocent woman of twenty-six given to reassuring smiles, a subdued voice, and a soft caressing touch. But there was a look in her eyes that had not been there before. Her hands moved more and her lips trembled slightly when she wasn't aware I was watching. Marie cried more and occasionally shivered during a warm sunny day, as if something cold was touching her, something from within that produced a chill she couldn't dispel. I first noticed the changes about a week ago, but said nothing. I knew she would eventually confide in me. We were engaged and shared everything, the good and the bad.

Last night she told me about the cave she had recently discovered. Her description started as if it was an ordinary, though unexpected, event. I waited and we relaxed. Her hesitation was apparent and she avoided looking directly into my eyes, quite unlike her usual behavior. We were sitting in front of a roaring fire, a friendly haven of warmth in my upscale apartment. Marie shivered and leaned in closer so I could envelop her with a blanket. She clutched her arms as if the fireplace was full of ice instead of burning logs.

"I can show you," Marie said. "I can take you there, it's close by. But Rod, you won't like it."

"Why not?" I reminded her that geology was a hobby of mine and caves ranked high on my list of places to visit. I was also unaware of any caves nearby. Both limestone caves and lava tubes were common in appropriate locales throughout Oregon, but not near our town. "How did you find it?"

"I decided to visit the cabin on my uncle's property, the land I inherited when he disappeared three years ago. He was presumed dead and the court finally issued papers to transfer the property to me. I knew about the old bungalow there, built sometime in the mid-nineteenth century, but I also knew the structure was a worthless derelict. The forty-acre property, however, would probably bring a decent price and I wanted to get a good look at it before listing it for sale."

§

The single room cabin had an old mattress, a small wooden table, and two chairs. The roof leaked in one corner and the wood underneath it was rotten. The door was ready to fall off its hinges and nearly did so when she opened it for the cursory inspection. The room gave no evidence of her uncle's presence. It was on her way back to the road that the dark crescent in the rock caught her eye. An old pine had snapped and fallen, flattening a large blackberry bush and exposing the top of a dark entrance into a basalt cliff. *Strange*, she thought. *No one in the family ever mentioned a cave in the cliff.*

Curious, Marie made her way cautiously through the bramble, but not without accumulating a number of scratches and a torn shirtsleeve. As she stepped past the bush, the full entrance was visible. It was about five feet high but extended back into darkness. She stepped inside and discovered a ceiling high enough to stand in comfortably. The floor near the entrance was smooth, yet appeared natural. Without a light, she knew she couldn't explore the cave further, but her desire to do so seemed more compelling than mere curiosity. It called to her somehow, an invitation to enter. She vowed to return when she was better prepared.

§

"Did you like the cave?"

She paused and answered slowly. "The cave is nothing special. It's just a hole in the ground until you are several feet inside. Then it changes—it becomes something else."

"Something else? What is *else*?"

"Like a large room, a place someone has built, but with cavern walls and ceiling. The place feels occupied, as if someone is there. And there's an entrance to another chamber in the cavern. The feeling is only a sensation, until you cross into the other room." She frowned.

"You've been back to it, after your initial discovery?"

"Yes. I wanted to see it again and explore the second room."

"Then what happened?" I was trying to be patient and continued to hold her as she shivered once again. She put her arms around my waist and buried her head against my chest.

94

"I love you," she said. "No matter what happens, I love you."

The way she said it troubled me. It wasn't a reassuring declaration, not offered in a manner that should have prompted a similar response. She said it as if saying goodbye, as if parting was inevitable. I prompted her to continue.

"I returned three days later," she said, "wearing jeans, sturdy boots, and a hardhat. I carried a machete and a flashlight. I thought about bringing a rope as well, but decided if that proved necessary, I'd return with you." She squeezed my hand and we exchanged smiles.

"At first, I thought of the cave as *my* place. That was odd, as if I had decided to keep it a secret from you. But we don't keep secrets, do we?" She looked at me for confirmation and I nodded. "I hacked a passageway through the berry bush, but not so wide as to make it visible to someone casually passing by. I wanted to keep the cave hidden until I knew what was in it, if anything." Another smile. I could tell Marie was a bit more assured.

"What did you think it might contain?" I asked. "Indian skeletons or the bones of ice age animals?"

She laughed and looked up at me. "Maybe loot from a bank or train robbery," she replied. "Maybe the cabin was the hideout of some old time crooks. The Old West still has some mysteries to solve. You never know." But then she became still and somber. "I might have found the remains of Uncle Charlie. But, no treasure, no signs of people or animals."

"Not even bats or rodents? Most western caves play host to something."

She paused. "I didn't see anything, not until I noticed the other entrance."

§

Marie turned her light on and stepped into the cave. The ceiling was higher than the entrance, about seven feet, and she could walk easily across the smooth floor. It was dry and cool, with no indication of a draft. She stepped further into the room, shining her light to the rear wall, about twenty feet away. That was when she first noticed the feeling, as if someone was in the cave watching her. It didn't feel threatening—it was just there, a sensation that she wasn't alone. She flashed the beam around the walls and discovered a five-foot entrance to another room at her right, near the rear wall.

"Is anyone here?" She asked in a quiet voice, feeling foolish as she did so. She didn't want an answer, but she had to ask. She was the intruder so she waited a few seconds before walking toward the entrance to the inner room, the space she would later call the "portal." As she neared the dark opening, the feeling of a presence grew, but now it changed in character. No longer just a vague impression of something coexisting in the space with her, it seemed like a magnet, drawing her toward the inner chamber, filling her with an irresistible desire to enter. At the same time, she could sense an undercurrent of dread growing, a warning to leave. She stopped two feet from the opening, flashing her light into the darkness, but nothing returned the beam, as if it was an endless void. *Not a very bright light*, she thought.

Despite her fear, the compulsion to discover any mysteries in the darkness was stronger. She stopped on the threshold of the entrance. *I'm not ready for this. I need a weapon of some kind, at least the machete I left at the entrance.*

Deciding to retrieve the blade, she turned and moved toward the entrance. As she did so, the sensations subsided. She picked up the machete, started to return to the inner doorway, but stopped, overcome by a wave of common sense. *I also need a stronger lamp and a camera.* She quickly left the cave, replaced a few branches across the opening, and went home, puzzled and somewhat shaken by her experience.

§

"And yet you returned?" I said.

"Yes, I returned, two days ago. I brought a small digital camera, LED flashlight, and my dad's 45 Ruger. I also did one other thing. I left a note in my apartment about where I had gone and how to find the cave. Just in case."

I must have frowned because she looked at me and gave me a playful punch in the stomach.

"Just in case I fell, sprained my ankle, you know, had trouble getting back."

"Yeah, dark bears in dark caves do things like that," I said, meaning it as a joke.

"I didn't smell a bear or any wild animal. In an enclosed space, there would have been a strong odor, even if the animal wasn't there at the time."

"You're probably right. So, then what?"

§

Marie entered the inner room, flashlight in her left hand, pistol in her right. Once again, she experienced the opposing sensations of her first visit, but when she crossed the threshold into the inner chamber, they stopped. She felt normal, as if she was outside of the cave. She looked around at the large space. The light barely reached the far walls to her left and right. The rear was still in darkness and the ceiling appeared to be twenty feet or more above her. But there was something in the center of the room, a raised platform of stone about fifteen feet from the entrance. It appeared to be a natural part of the cave floor, which was smooth rock like the outer chamber.

As she approached the platform, she placed the gun in her holster, but kept her right hand near it, ready to draw if necessary. There was a large crystal sphere, about five or six inches in diameter, at the center of the platform, too well placed to be natural. The sphere reflected a shimmering golden color from the light. The height of the almost circular platform came to mid-chest and the width was about six feet across. The near walls appeared to be dark basalt in natural patterns of lava flow. The far wall was still shrouded in shadow. The platform with its jeweled centerpiece was the only feature of the room she could see.

She set the flashlight down on the edge of the platform and bent closer to the crystal. Although roughly spherical and appearing to be a natural mineral, the object was incongruous with the setting. As she leaned further forward and her head crossed an invisible extension of the platform edge, Marie became aware of a whispering noise, resembling the sound of water spilling over rocks backed by a vocal chorus, chanting without distinct words. She pulled back, standing erect, and the noise stopped. She leaned forward again, and the sound resumed, as if it was coming from some distance but echoing through the large chamber. She carefully reached toward the crystal with her left hand. She had to stretch the full length of her arm and lean her body across the platform to reach it. As she did, the volume of the rushing sound increased, filling the chamber. She stopped without touching the rock and once again withdrew.

Something is triggering the noise, associated with my presence at the platform. She didn't recognize the type of crystal, but realized it was probably unique and potentially important. *I need to tell Rod about this.*

She picked up the flashlight, turned on her heels and started toward the inner chamber door. A wave of nausea enveloped her immediately and she staggered, almost dropping the light. Gasping, she stopped—the sickness eased but didn't disappear. She stepped toward the opening again and it returned, only stronger and accompanied by an overwhelming sense of dread, as if leaving the room was the worst possible action she could take. Again, she paused, considering what to do. *Can I make it to the doorway? Should I move slowly and try to endure or should I make a run for it and throw myself through the portal?* Believing she would be safe once she was in the outer chamber, she steeled herself, grabbed the light with both hands, and ran at full speed for the inner entrance.

The fear intensified as she reached the opening, pounding her with an unbearable mix of horror and revulsion. Her legs wanted to freeze, to paralyze and prevent her from leaving. She made it past the threshold only by ignoring her heaving stomach and by sheer desperation. In the outer chamber, she collapsed on the floor and vomited. Only then did she feel physical relief and the absence of mental anxiety. The outer entrance beckoned. She quickly stood and walked out of the cave, not bothering to brush off her clothes until she was a few feet from the entrance.

That was when she discovered she no longer had the pistol. *It must have come out of the holster when I fell to the floor.* Wanting to go back in and retrieve it, she couldn't force herself to reenter the cave. *I'll get it later, after I have time to recover. As long as I don't enter the second room, I should be okay.* As she walked back to her car, she thought, *is this horrible discomfort only mine or will other people feel it?*

Marie didn't sleep that night. The feelings returned as she tossed and turned, although not as intense. Rod was out of town, but she decided she could enter the outer chamber and retrieve the pistol. The next day, she did so without incident, experiencing only the slight push-pull feelings of the first day. She glanced toward the inner opening, the portal to the jewel, but didn't go near it.

§

After Marie finished her story, I told her I'd like to see the geode, or whatever it was, and explore the rest of the inner cavern. "There might be other things, maybe other rooms beyond where the light fell," I said.

"But the feeling, the sickness, I don't know if I could stand that again—it almost stopped me. I might have been trapped inside of the cave, unable to move." She was looking at me, her nervousness at the prospect of returning to the cave visible in her hands, shaking slightly again. Her eyes were moist as I held and tried to reassure her.

"There will be two of us," I explained. "I'll go in first to see if it has the same effect. You can watch from the outer chamber and get help if I can't make it out." Her look of alarm was immediate. "But, I'll make it out. If I have the same feelings, we should know it in the outer chamber, right?"

Although I smiled with confidence, I also knew Marie wasn't prone to hysteria or baseless fears. Something had scared her and worse. That, and the mysterious jewel, only made the quest seem that much more necessary. We decided we would go together on the weekend.

§

Saturday morning dawned bright and clear, not a cloud in the sky. September on the wooded high plains near the base of the Cascades always seemed brisk and more refreshing than at any other time. Marie and I prepared a light lunch, brought rope, and we each had a miner's headlamp so we could keep our hands free. I had a large Bowie knife strapped to my belt and Marie had the holster and Ruger, "just in case." If possible, I wanted to walk well back into the inner chamber. Marie wasn't sure about this, even if the sickness didn't reappear.

The cave was about a hundred yards from the dirt road. We parked my Jeep in a small clearing and hiked in together. We had left notes at our respective apartments to indicate where we were. I also told Keith, my best friend, about Marie's experience and what we planned to do. Our unanswered question concerned the mineral on the platform. Should we bring it back? More importantly, could we bring it back? Marie had never touched it. Her hand was still a few inches short of contact when she decided to retreat. My longer reach should remedy that, but with what result? I brought a lined plastic bag and some bubble wrap in case the mineral was fragile.

We neared the entrance, removed the loose branches, and walked into the outer chamber, stopping a few feet inside.

"Do you feel anything?" I asked.

"Just a little, mostly a pleasant hint of attraction, like a place I am comfortable in." She shuddered, commenting on how different it was on the other side of the threshold. "There it is, the other chamber." Her light revealed the portal as she pointed. I watched her beam play across the edges of the entrance. Only blackness beckoned on the other side. "How are you feeling…anything?" She looked at me, searching for some sign that I was sharing her experience.

"Some excitement, anticipation, I guess. But no, I can't say I am feeling anything positive or negative." A pause. "Shall we proceed?"

"I love you Rod." She lowered her head and stepped closer so we could touch. Once again, she said it as if she was sending me off to war, quiet and fearful. I squeezed her hand and stepped back.

We walked toward the inner portal. I was two steps in front of Marie and stopped at the threshold to look back at her. She gave me a weak smile. "Feel okay?" I asked and she nodded, but her anxiety was apparent.

I stepped across the threshold as my light revealed the platform and the golden crystal. Marie stood on the other side of the portal, watching me. I took two more steps toward the platform and felt suddenly as if the platform was inviting me forward to learn its secret. I looked back at Marie, but she stood motionless, hands at her sides, as if resigned to whatever fate awaited us. Turning back to the platform, I walked forward with a long decisive stride.

The geode gleamed and shimmered as the headlight beam crossed its surface. The shimmer was particularly mesmerizing and most unusual for a crystal, as if the structure was moving like a liquid. My left hand held the plastic bag, open and ready to receive the treasure. As I reached forward, a murmur of voices rose. As Marie had described, I couldn't make out distinct words, more like nonsense syllables that increased in volume as my hand touched the crystal. The rock was cold, very cold. I lifted it easily from the platform surface and wrapped the bubble pack material around it. I placed the crystal carefully in the bag, sealing it. The noise increased in volume and in pitch.

As I turned, I saw Marie take one step inside the chamber, but she immediately lunged back into the outer chamber. Mindful of her experience, I started quickly for the portal as she watched with an open mouth. I stumbled but kept my feet as an intense paralysis and fear clutched at me. I was sick and could barely see the entrance, but kept moving, understanding that hesitation could mean disaster. Five feet, less than a body length from the threshold, I bent over double, the pain in my stomach blinding me to everything else.

Marie ran to me and pulled me toward the entrance, ignoring her own discomfort. We collapsed in the outer chamber, in each other's arms, sick and vomiting. Panting to catch my breath, I could feel the stomach cramps easing, but it took me a full minute to stretch out and stand up. Marie remained sitting, her arms wrapped around her knees. She was mumbling something to herself.

"What did you say?" I asked, kneeling and putting my arm around her.

"I said, was it worth it?" She looked up at me and slowly rose to her feet. "Maybe we should have left it in there. Maybe we made a mistake."

"Too late now, I'm not going back. We have it. Let's get it analyzed at the State Museum and find out what this is." I put the plastic bag in my backpack.

"Listen, Rod, I can still hear the noise from the inner room." She cocked her head to one side.

"Yeah, but it's not near as loud out here as it was in there, even though the entrance is open. It's like a doorway to…*what*?" She was staring at me, like I had missed the point of her comment. I had.

"Rod, when I was here alone, the noise stopped as soon as I crossed the threshold. It was silent out here, as if nothing had happened. Is it because we have the crystal?"

"I don't know, but let's go. The farther from this cave, the better, at least for today." We walked back to the car in silence, but both of us could hear a very slight murmur, as if we were experiencing a strange form of tinnitus.

§

The hallucinations started that evening, after we finished dinner at Marie's apartment. Marie didn't want to be alone, not even for a few minutes. The murmur was still there, a background noise that had not abated. I called it an "after tone," something similar to an after image from staring at a bright light. Marie kept shaking her head, whether to try and clear the noise or to make sense of what had happened, I wasn't sure.

We put on some light music, opened a bottle of wine, and tried to relax. The mineral sat on the kitchen table under a light, but the crystals seemed dull, more like the color of old urine. There was no glitter, no shimmer. At eleven, we climbed into bed, tired but not at ease.

The first dream woke Marie just after midnight. Screaming and holding her head, she threw up on me and started crying. I had dreamed also but not as vividly. The stomach cramps returned, but I wasn't sick. I took Marie into the bathroom, removed our bedclothes, and we took a quick shower. The murmur had now risen to a dull roar and we had to speak in loud, clear voices to be understood.

"This is crazy. What is happening to us?" she said, in between sobs as I dried her off.

"I don't know. Whatever it is, it seems you are more sensitive to it than I am. I can feel it, everything you described, but it isn't as bad as what you're experiencing."

"I dreamt about my uncle," she said. "I could see his face—it was blurry, but his hand—it was reaching toward me, almost touching me, as if he was trying to…I don't know, warn me, push me back." She sobbed and buried her head in my chest as I held her. After sitting for a while, we decided to try again for sleep. The symptoms had lessened and we were both exhausted. Sleep came in fits and starts, interrupted by dreams, but not as dramatic as before.

At breakfast the next morning, Marie told me she wanted to take the crystal back to the cave.

"Marie, after what we went through to get it out? You can't be serious. Let's identify it first, then make a decision." I reached across the table and took her hand. "I know this has been really rough for you, but we have it. Besides, I'm not sure either of us is strong enough to face the inner room again."

"Oh, Rod, I know, I know. It is a nightmare and the nightmare is still with us. It followed us home. How will this end?" Her look was pleading, searching for an answer, for a solution I didn't have. Finally, she said in a husky low voice that I barely recognized, "I love you Rod. I always will, no matter what."

I nodded, squeezed her hand, and told her the effects should eventually lessen and then disappear, as if I knew what I was talking about. I told her, if it was important enough, other people could enter the cave and solve the mystery of the place and the psychotic images it generated. I kissed her and left at eleven to bring Keith back to inspect the sphere.

§

By eleven thirty, the noises had grown louder again, but without nausea or fear. Marie kept staring at the dull yellow crystal on the table and became increasingly obsessed with taking it back to the cave. She didn't want to spend another night like the last one. At noon, she picked it up, stuck it in the plastic bag and walked out to her Corolla. *This might be my only chance to end this nightmare before I go completely crazy.*

She drove quickly to the dirt road, got out, and walked to the cave entrance. She cleared the entrance and entered the outer chamber, recognizing the feeling of attraction and familiar comfort. Turning on her headlamp, she walked to the threshold and stood there, gazing at the empty platform in the light beam.

§

Keith and I returned to the Marie's house a few minutes after noon. The first thing I noted was Marie's car was missing. *Probably went out to get something for dinner tonight.* I entered the house and took Keith into the kitchen. The vacant space on the kitchen table told me all I needed to know.

"She's taking it back, damn it, we need to stop her."

We raced outside for the Jeep. I drove quickly to the dirt road and parked next to Marie's car. Jumping out, I ran toward the cave, Keith close at my heels. When we entered the outer chamber, Marie was standing at the portal, as if in a trance.

"Marie, wait, don't go in," I shouted. We walked quickly up to the threshold. I took the mineral from Marie and showed it briefly to Keith.

Marie grabbed my arm. "No, I need to put it back. *Now!*" The urgency in her voice indicated that it wasn't up for discussion. I nodded to Keith and took the crystal from his hands.

"We'll put it back, together. Keith can wait out here, in case we need his help." Keith nodded, obviously disappointed about returning the rock. "We can always get help with this later, from professionals that are better prepared than us." I smiled at Marie and indicated where Keith was to stand and watch.

The background murmur was pleasant as we held the crystal in front of us, the geode sparkling and shimmering as before. I gently placed the rock at the center of the platform as Marie's lamp lit the scene. The return glare from the crystal was almost blinding and the murmur rose to a crescendo— then there was silence. We looked briefly around the room and turned for the run back to the portal. After two quick steps, we realized that there was no pain, no feeling of dread or horror. We stopped and looked back at the crystal. Was it over? Had we redeemed ourselves by returning it?

Relieved, we turned once more to the doorway—the disappearing doorway. As we watched, the opening quickly shrank. We rushed to where the portal had been and touched the surface. No trace of an opening, as if it had never been. Dazed by the discovery, it took us a few moments to realize that the chamber was shrinking, the surrounding space becoming progressively smaller. The platform was now only a few feet away and we could see the back wall. It looked like a large plate glass window, from floor to ceiling. Marie's light reflected from its surface.

The platform was now touching our legs. The rock table and the geode were the only things in the room not growing smaller. As the platform pushed against us, we fell onto it, to lie beside the glittering geode. Marie and I looked up to see the ceiling descend and the walls envelop us, enclosing us in the void, the blackness within. Our final words of goodbye merged with the rising chant of others—so many others.

§

Keith watched in dismay as the opening to the inner chamber shrank to nothing, becoming part of the featureless wall. He called out but could hear nothing from the other side. He ran quickly out of the cave to seek help. Looking back at the entrance, he was shocked to see that it had disappeared. Not a trace, as if the cave had never been there. Maybe it hadn't. He wasn't sure. When he approached the road, he saw two cars parked, a Jeep and a Toyota. *Not mine*, he thought. *Must have walked here.* He couldn't remember, things were fuzzy, as if it had happened in a dream that was already fading.

Capture is complete, indicated the first observer behind the glass window.

It appears we captured two of them, answered the second observer. *We were only after the female.*

No problem. The chorus is diverse and there will be places for more in the future. Restore the chamber.

Stephen Hagelin wrote his first novel at the age of nine, and by the time he reached adulthood, had written several more. Writing was always his first love, though he got a BA in Japanese at the University of Washington and studied engineering for several years. He is currently working on The Commission Series, of which the first two novels have been released, *The Venomsword* and *The Viper's Chase*.

DOOR INTO THE DUCK DIMENSION

Stephen Hagelin

Monroe Magical Academy
The Basement

H arriet stood with her folded hands in front of her, fidgeting, but not from any sort of anxiety about passing her practicum. She eyed her rival, anxious to perform at least as well as she did. For in all things, magic and make-up, Mary excelled—and she was barely two months older! She gave Harriet a condescending smile, tilting her head back proudly, staring down her pointy nose, her blue eyes flashing, her blond hair perfect, as she patted her black lab, Berlin.

Harriet lifted a hand to toss her dark curls over her shoulder, freeing her brilliantly colored mallard duck, where he was perched and preening conscientiously. Feathers was her familiar, servant, and assistant in her pursuits as a fledgling hedgewitch. His webbed foot dangled near her neck, his ample belly spilling over her shoulder, as he pulled a winter feather from his back and tossed it away with a cheerful, soft quack. Mary watched it drift to the ground with a look of distaste.

Their younger classmate, Jose, scrunched his freckled nose as he seemed about to sneeze. He didn't. The child was very proper, and talented, and as he waited for the test to begin, he fished out a bit of dried mango from his pocket and chewed on its end.

"This *basement* needs air conditioning," Feathers commented in a dry hushed quack.

Harriet snickered, but gulped when she received a stern glare from her instructor.

Mary bore the interruption with a deadpan expression, betraying nothing. Jose didn't seem to notice or mind her laughter, as he stared with all the devotion one would expect of a future master wizard, his brown eyes glistening with the precocious piety of the most academic student, gazing up at their…master…Jack Malwitch. But then, he *was* only 9.

What does he even see in this Geriatric Wonder? Harriet thought to herself, scratching Feather's neck absently.

Jack began. "Dimensional magic is the foundational study of all wizards," he proposed, to which they all nodded, more to encourage him to keep talking than from agreement, "for it allows the witch or wizard to summon friendly familiars, or to travel long distances in a hurry."

Harriet rolled her eyes, knowing that he was about to go off on another tangent.

"Why in my student days at Cascadia Community College, I used to eat breakfast at my parents' house in Sultan five minutes before my trigonometry class and then waltz through the Interstitial Space to sneak in through the door while she called attendance!" Feathers burped, but Jack smiled kindly, and brushed a stray hair behind his ear.

"My…uh, *a* familiar, actually, was one I found by accident on one such excursion, this time heading to Washington State History, when I happened upon a memory of the forests before Bothell became as large as it is today."

"How large is it today?" she whispered to Mary, earning a silencing elbow jab and a choked laugh.

"And in my haste, I tripped and fell headlong into an overgrown fern! Even though I was soon covered in dirt and leaves, and twigs, and…and… pollen, I think, and I heard a strange, small voice! 'Can you get off of me?' it said, and so of course, I stood up and looked in the bushes and in that depression I had created, I saw one of those black and orange caterpillars, the fuzzy ones—a Dreamworm! It was a little flattened but being only the *memory* of a butterfly, it couldn't really be harmed, so it scootched over toward me and looked hard at me with what I think were its eyes."

You're that certain, are you? she marveled, glancing at her watch. *This is going to take the whole class!*

Jack looked off to the side, as if still lost in that dream, clasping his hands together as he continued. "'Do you often go tramping through people's memories?' it demanded. I admitted that I didn't, and that I was on my way to school. But in all this excitement, I was running even later for class, and had gotten lost in that forest. So, I asked for directions, and she didn't want to give them to me."

Why would she, after you sat on her?

"…and so I picked her up and put her on my shoulder and started backtracking. She grudgingly told me where the exit was and asked to be put down, and well…I was so late already, I forgot to do so, and so I entered my classroom with a Dreamworm on my shoulder and was granted a sharp look from my instructor! I got away with it though, because I used the memories of Bothell's past to describe some of the city's history to my teacher to explain I'd gotten pulled into the reading..."

Mary ground her teeth, her patience obviously used up.

"Dimensional travel is useful in so many inexplicable ways!" he exclaimed at last, taking a few long breaths to recover from his monologue.

Jose raised an eyebrow at him. "Do you still have your familiar, or did she turn into a Dreamfly?"

Jack's brightly lit face fell, and he sighed. "She returned to her dreams the moment she could fly." He deflated further as he said it, his shoulders slumping in relived resignation.

None of this was relevant to their examinations, but then, Harriet wouldn't object to further delays either. She reached up and scratched Feathers' neck, mumbling to herself, "It's a wonder he ever got out of there with an associate of arts..."

Feathers tutted as only a bird could, and said, "Natural studies aside, Harriet, he is still a moderately accomplished wizard, *and* your instructor. It does no good to belittle him and call him a 'geriatric' has-been or worse. Besides, he's only 35."

35, yes, geriatric, though not in the usual *sense.* Jack worked at a senior home, and on Tuesdays and Thursdays, he taught the local witches and wizards as best he could.

Jose grinned, interrupting gently, "I only just popped in for the test, Mr. Malwitch." Harriet sneered, but covered it quickly as Feathers nipped at her earlobe chidingly.

Jack froze, mid-sentence, as he realized the significance of the child's utterance. "A...all already?" he confirmed awkwardly, as if he couldn't believe his prized pupil was capable of mastering the intricacies of dimensional magic at such a young age.

The boy nodded seriously, shoving his hands in his pockets proudly.

Mary stiffened, but relaxed when her Black Stallion of a dog nuzzled her hand with his nose, and she locked her brilliant, blue, haughty eyes with Harriet's. "Jose is a talented wizard, Mr. Malwitch, that is why he was inducted into our school, isn't that right?"

Harriet bit her tongue. Talent had *nothing* to do with any of this. Malwitch was simply the *only* "qualified" wizard in Snohomish County— the dolt could hardly help himself, much less his students, amount to anything. There was nothing for it though, Harriet's parents still thought he was tutoring her in calculus...fat lot of good that would do, or would have done, for her, but there it was. He "taught" them magic from the glorious auspices of his mother's basement! *Academy* indeed!

"Of course, Mary," Jack said with a self-satisfied smile, as if she'd been complimenting him. "Jose, will you go first?" he asked, bobbing foolishly as he directed their attention toward a mirror-less, once-ornate frame that accented a view of a cobwebbed, concrete foundation wall in tarnished silver scrollwork. Jose seemed to understand what their instructor wanted, but Harriet frowned, and grimaced when Feathers quacked in her ear in a low warning.

"Don't worry," he rasped, in a confident tone, "I can help you cast this door. Did you bring the materials?"

Harriet swallowed, and muttered, "two seagull feathers, an empty snail shell, two cat-eye marbles, um…and…uh…" She produced the articles in her shaking hands, reluctantly handling the last, unmentionable item.

"A slug!" He honked excitedly, loud enough to make her flinch, but not loud enough to alarm her classmates. He snaked his head out of her dark, curly hair, and narrowed his eyes at the boy, who had not obtained a familiar yet. "I am curious to see *his* progress too."

Underlying his tone was the hint that he expected more from her. That was hardly a familiar's job, but in a way, she was grateful, since Jack only occasionally seemed to recognize her presence, let alone her talent. Mary, had secured their teacher's eye; she looked older than her 21 years for one, and she had an intelligent and socially acceptable familiar… No one, no matter how naturalistic, expected someone to have a pet duck—especially one who typically perched on a shoulder, or bore an affronted look when he was taken for a waddle on a leash. Perhaps he recognized her talents because she pretended to listen to him?

Jose snapped his fingers and cast a sprinkle of ashes and grass cuttings at the frame, as a split-second flash of light flicked from his thumb and forefinger, and the thrown items disintegrated into dust. His lips moved silently, and a shimmering light realized itself into the dimensions of the mirror, forming into a spiraling swirl of gray smoke that was shot through with dried leaf flakes, and sparks and embers that wouldn't die out. A hot, arid wind flowed out of the mirror, but the basement was silent.

Jack gulped.

They all stared spellbound and even Jose's eyes widened with wonder, as one of the glowing sparks flew through the mirror, and fell, radiant and warm, to the floor. A pulsing orange light flowed from it, growing dimmer and redder with each second. They all leaned closer to inspect it…a piece of fire, a grain of hot sand that refused to simply go cold. Jose stepped closer and crouched before it, holding his small hand close to test its heat. Despite the shimmering air around it, he tentatively gave it a light pat. But it shrank back like a cat from an icy hand and resolved into a glimmering curled form of low-burning flames.

Jose persisted in touching its back, and slowly pet its fiery coat, from neck to trailing tail, till a warm 'purr' resonated from the Embercat.

Feathers would have whistled, Harriet sensed, but his beak would not permit such a sound, instead he clicked, and bobbed his head as he looked at his own noticeably drab and dirty feathers.

"An Embercat is a rare familiar to obtain, Harriet, but he must give it a name to change its form," he commented hopefully. What he hoped for, she couldn't say.

She rolled her eyes. "Naming *you* did hardly anything."

He kind of shriveled a bit. "A spirit duck is still a duck. An Embercat, well, is still basically a cat. It's just a little on fire," he added with a huff.

Jack observed Jose petting the Embercat with his jaw hanging dumbly open, and even Mary was taken aback. She scratched Berlin's ears muttering a few nervous '*who's a good boy*'s out of reflex. Harriet sighed, impressed despite her displeasure with the boy's progress. In a few months, he'd probably overtake Mr. Malwitch and become their tutor…oh, *that'd* be rich.

"You're a pretty nice kitty, aren't you?" Jose asked, coaxing the cat's chin up to be scratched, as its flame-tongue whiskers pricked up and it rose to its feet to arch its back and stretch. It purred loudly, with a hint of the crackle of a fire in its voice.

"Cats can tell who's nice, and who to avoid, kid," the cat replied at last, "you're not so bad."

Jose smiled wide, and picked up the cat, resting it over his shoulder. "I think I'll call you Don," he said, "you want to be my familiar?"

"Hmm…" he purred, "only if you feed me twice a day, brush my coat, and clean up the ash…but what kind of name is Don?"

"Don Quixote," he answered, "a little odd, but an honorable man."

"Hmph," Don sniffed, "that's not bad." He swished his smoke-and-fire tail and the portal to the ember-world faded, vanishing without even leaving a smell.

Jack was stunned. He had watched all this with disbelief, but now he simply was at a loss. Harriet was sure that any more of this kind of shock would render him catatonic—and almost hoped it would. "W…well done, Jose, you've done very well indeed. I will need to instruct you on more advanced topics." He gulped, possibly because he wasn't qualified to instruct anyone in anything more advanced. "Mary, if you please, could you demonstrate for us a dimensional portal?"

"Easily," she simpered, gliding forward in an exaggeratedly "feminine" gait. Berlin, the dog, cantered up after her and sat dutifully in front of the mirror. Mary opened an envelope and cast a sprinkle of glitter, a few strands of hair, and a dash of smoked sea salt at the mirror frame, invoking a few whispered words. Unfortunately, the materials for her casting were not consumed as Jose's had been, but instead seemed to multiply before and behind the frame, as it resolved into a translucent membrane not unlike the skin of a soap bubble, or a watery pudding.

The Embercat snorted or sneezed, and stared daggers at the dog, as fluffs of dander and shed hair floated out of the other side of the portal. Berlin pretended not to notice, but his tail stopped wagging, and he hung his head slightly.

Mary turned and presented her portal with a proud, magician's assistant sort of hand-wave, "This is my room!"

Indeed, Harriet could not have imagined such an overly glamoured bedroom for her rival to have. It was obvious, though she'd tried to hide it, that some assembly had been required. The view through their inter-dimensional window revealed lacy, pastel-colored quilts on a queen-sized bed, with her potion ingredients arrayed on a shelf over a tiny white desk, that carefully displayed her rarely-used alembics, and marble mortar and pestle. There was a magnificent dog bed in the corner, and flowers growing outside her window. Barely visible through it was a view of her neighbors' house, sprinklers were watering the lawn, and a man pushed a lawnmower in the distance. It was horrible. Was she trying to rub it in? Jose's family was pretty poor, Harriet's parents taught music for a pittance, and Jack… well…perhaps he was worst off of all. He observed the scene through the mirror as if he were watching an iconic drama from the fifties: some kind of make-believe idyllic scene of American prosperity before the bursting of their economic and illusory bubble, now observable through the soapy skin on this silver frame.

He shivered and looked away. "Yes, very well done, Mary." He retreated a few steps, rubbing the back of his neck for a minute or so. Harriet stood there, forgotten, watching her tutor with a newfound sense of pity. Not enough to forgive him for being her instructor perhaps, but enough to prick her conscience a little.

Feathers shifted uncomfortably on her shoulder and fluttered down to the base of the mirror. His head snaked around, and he narrowed his eyes at her. "Come along Harriet," he said softly.

Harriet obeyed, approaching the mirror with the same kind of trepidation that she'd felt when she attempted to summon a familiar—like feeling nauseous but hungry at the same time, with a dry throat, and a hot prickle on her scalp. She reached deep into the pocket of her denim jacket and pulled out the inoffensive items required to create this portal, and then in the opposite pocket, she withdrew the ziplock bag with the slug; which unfortunately had only grown longer and grosser in the bag. Taking a deep breath, she dumped everything into the bag, shook it up to coat the slug in the feathers, the shell, and the rest, and then turned it inside out and dropped the slug on the ground, with a moist splat.

Feathers stepped over, pecked at it with his beak, tossed it into the air, and caught it, swallowing it whole in a sickening, gagging display. Finally, he sort of coughed, and blew a foul-smelling breath at the mirror, fluffing up his feathers as a tremulous doorway appeared within the imaginary glass.

A soft breezed drifted toward them, and on it the gentle sound of rustling leaves, and the mild ripple of a creek emptying into a pool. They all stared through the initial mist, and then, had varying responses to the sight.

Feathers turned 'round proudly, expanding his wings. Harriet blushed, as she realized just *what* her duck had summoned. Mary scoffed, and then covered it with a chuckle. Jose was silent, though Don's purr intensified as if he were about to chase down some prey.

Jack let out a sigh. One of those disappointed, yet resigned sort of sighs, the kind a parent gives when their child takes fifth in a six-person footrace or forgets to fill in the circles for their answers on the SATs.

Cheerful quacking carried outwards, and Feathers nearly flew through the mirror to join his family, who were gathered on a tree-shaded pond filled with ducks swimming and diving, or flying, or landing upon its surface. The grass around the banks was thoroughly trampled, muddied, and littered with droppings, and a sickly-sweet smell oozed from the other side.

Harriet snapped her fingers to close the doorway, but nothing happened, so she snapped again, and then again, as she got redder and redder in the face. "Feathers!? What have you done?"

He turned sharply in alarm. "Why I have made this a permanent portal! Aren't you pleased?"

Despite her horror, Harriet *was* impressed. It was just a shame that his permanent portal opened to a duck pond, instead of something useful, like a hot spring, or the gym. Mary burst out laughing uncontrollably, bending over and holding her stomach as Berlin barked in agreement.

The Embercat curled up on top of Jose's head and fell asleep, no longer interested, causing Jose to smile.

Her tutor was silent as he approached the mirror with a childlike, blank expression, and stepped into the Duck Dimension. He found a large rock next to the pond, and plopped down, resting his elbows on his knees, and his chin in his hands. His shoulders sagged, and his eyes grew watery, and he pondered the ducks.

Jose shrugged and left the basement, with Mary leaving soon after. Harriet and Feathers followed Mr. Malwitch through the mirror, standing at a respectful distance.

"Did you bring any breadcrumbs?" Feathers asked, licking his beak.

She shot him a mean look. "You're hungry even after eating that slug?"

He shook his head sagely. "I meant for him." He bobbed his head in the direction of her teacher and set to work cleaning his feathers.

Jack now held his face in his hands, coming to terms with poverty, the ennui of the unaccomplished, and the futility of study, all at once. With a pang of regret for thinking so badly of him, Harriet walked over. Remembering a small pouch of bread crumbs in her pocket, she withdrew it uncertainly, and held the bag out before him.

She coughed gently, giving it a small shake.

His teary eyes lit on the bag of crumbs like a man facing eviction staring at a wad of cash, and he accepted it without a word. He opened his mouth, and then closed it again, and she had the impression he'd said 'thanks,' but couldn't be sure.

"See you Thursday, Mr. Malwitch." She walked away, biting her lip in thought.

A soft splash announced the first dash of crumbs on the pond. And a quiet, choked sob was swallowed, as the first duck devoured the bread.

"If you have some dried maple leaves and pine needles, maybe we could go visit the Dreamfly, and see if she'll come back?" Feathers suggested. "What is a wizard without a familiar?"

Harriett bristled at that, but relaxed, when she glanced back over her shoulder at her teacher again—hollow, and alone. She took a resigned breath and let it out again slowly. "Alright, if you think it'll help."

He quacked happily.

"But only because he's no use to us like *that*."

He quacked knowingly.

Jonathan Eaton grew up in Texas in the 20th century, moved to Oregon in the 21st century, and mostly writes about Texas in the 19th and 25th centuries. He is the author of the western novels *A Good Man for an Outlaw* and *Outlaws and Worse*. He is married to a percussionist named Cyndi, and, when it's rainy or cold outside, he has a cat named Sherman.

WHERE THE GRAPES OF HAPPINESS ARE STORED

Jonathan Eaton

In 2039, Harlan Hazlet, perhaps the greatest viticulturist the world has ever known, had a plan to keep the Oregon wine industry one step ahead of global warming. He developed a breed of grape especially suited to growing on the cool flanks of Mt. Hood. But just as the first harvest of his test acre was about to begin, the old volcano roared suddenly back to life, erupting for the first time in 132 years. Harlan was not a man easily deterred. He single-handedly dug the vineyard out from under fifteen feet of ash, even as the mountain continued to rumble and shake menacingly. The vines were done for, but Harlan found the grapes not only undamaged, but miraculously improved for having been cuddled for some weeks in the warm embrace of mineral ash. The ash was not so kind to Harlan Hazlet. The crushed grapes were still cooling in the fermenting tub when Hazlet was diagnosed with a terminal case of pneumoconiosis, or "ash lung." Harlan lived just long enough to have a taste of the wine he had sacrificed his life to bring to fruition. He took one sip before he died, and his last words were: "It was damn well worth it."

Only the lawyers handling Hazlet's estate know for sure what happened to those few precious bottles of "Oregon Happiness Red" after Hazlet's death, but there is a rumor that the entirety of the vintage was purchased, for several hundreds of millions of dollars, by the eccentric and reclusive self-made billionaire, oenophile, and inventor of the teleportation platform, Hester Murrow.

§

At three minutes before seven pm, Laura Spoonts, who had been containing herself all day, could contain herself no longer, and told her husband, Percival Spoonts, exactly what she thought of the man he had invited to dine with them that evening.

"I know Blane Chillingsworth is rude, and a horrible snob," Percival Spoonts said, "but he is a powerful man at Celestial Investments, and when I first found employment there, he took me under his wing, and he continues to look out for me to this day. It is a relationship that it is in my interest—in *our* interest—to cultivate. And Laura, I do believe there is some good in him, and he's lonely, and he considers me a friend."

"He looks out for you because he knows your worth—your hard work makes him look good. And he only accepts our dinner invitations because he knows you keep a well-stocked and intriguingly eclectic wine cellar."

"So you're saying he is a man of great discernment?"

"Humph," Laura Spoonts said, and was about to say more, when their conversation was cut short by the entrance of Alloy Bob, announcing the arrival of Blane Chillingsworth.

"At least he's punctual," Percival said. "Alloy Bob, please escort Mr. Chillingsworth to the dining room."

"Yes, Mr. Spoonts."

"I have some news," Chillingsworth said, when all three were seated at the table. "I have recently remarried. For the…six, seven, eight…*ninth* time, I think."

"I had no idea," Percival said, "you didn't say anything. Congratulations."

"Thank you."

"Anyone we know?" Laura asked.

"No," Chillingsworth replied. "No one you know."

"Where did you meet her?"

"Meet her? A showroom, I suppose you would call it. You see, I finally realized why none of my previous marriages ever lasted more than a year or two. Though my ex-wives all loved me enough, and were strong enough, to scale an immense mountain of flaws in order to overlook them, when they reached the lofty peak, all they saw from that vantage point was another, even higher, mountain of flaws. No *real* woman could ever put up with me for long. But my new bride, Laconia, won't have that problem. She has been customized to accept me just the way I am. What a real woman would find an intolerable shortcoming, Laconia embraces as an endearing quirk. Yes, my friends, it's true: I have married a machine, or as the salesman called it, a 'synthetic individual.' And Laconia looks and acts so human, I swear, I often forget that she is not. She laughs at my jokes, and when I'm feeling down, she comforts me, and a tear will roll down her cheek, in sympathy with my own. I suppose it is not really a sympathetic tear, but only a synthetic tear. I suppose she feels nothing at all, but on the other hand, who knows? They are so sophisticated now. I am certain they understand us much better than we understand them—or even ourselves! Perhaps they have feelings like ours, or no feelings at all, or feelings so *un*like ours they are beyond our comprehension—but feelings, nonetheless. I wonder if Laconia will pretend to grieve for me when I die, or if the charade will end the nanosecond I shuffle off this mortal coil."

"I could never love a machine," Laura said.

"Oh, I think you could," Chillingsworth said. "In fact, I think you do. Your poor old Alloy Bob is long overdue for a well-earned rest in the scrapyard, but you don't have the heart to exchange him for a newer model, do you? There's no shame in it. After all, hasn't it been human nature for all of time to love most those who cannot—or will not—love us in return?"

Just then Alloy Bob came into the dining room carrying a covered silver platter. The silver lid rattled on the silver tray like an introductory roll on a snare drum. Had the effect been intentional, it would have been both clever and funny, but it wasn't intentional, and therefore, neither clever nor funny, but only sad, as it was an indication of the increasing difficulty Alloy Bob was having with the fine-motion sub-controller unit in his left shoulder.

"Might be time to consider a new occupation for Alloy Bob," Chillingsworth said.

"A new occupation?" Laura Spoonts said.

"Yes," Chillingsworth replied, "I believe you could rent him out to entertain children."

"You mean he could be a clown or put on puppet shows?"

"No, Mrs. Spoonts," Chillingsworth said, "I mean he could be the titular 'can' in games of 'kick the can.' "

Percival forced out a ha-ha, earning him a look of severe disapproval from his wife. When he mouthed the question *what?* Laura closed her eyes and shook her head, a gesture Percival read as forgiveness but was something closer to annoyed resignation.

"Now," Chillingsworth said, "let's see what your fine collection of obsolete hardware and unsupported software has cooked up for us tonight." Chillingsworth leaned forward and lifted the silver lid. "Oh, I say—well done old chip! Steamed rondure of dubsfubble!"

"Mr. Spoonts told me it was your favorite," Alloy Bob said.

"Did he now? Well bless Mr. Spoonts for his thoughtfulness."

Chillingsworth set the silver lid back on the tray and turned towards Percival. "I am reminded of an amusing incident," Chillingsworth said. "I recently ordered a steamed rondure of dubsfubble at my favorite restaurant, and they brought me roasted instead. Well, I was terribly put off, as you can imagine, but as I was in something of a hurry, I ate it anyway. And do you know, Percy, I now believe that *roasted* rondure of dubsfubble is far superior to steamed. Roasting truly brings out the flavor. But since we have steamed, we shall make do with steamed. I know you consider yourself something of a wine connoisseur, Percy, and have a well-stocked cellar, so I shall follow your recommendation. What would you say pairs well with a steamed rondure of dubsfubble?"

A decanter of wine, and the bottle it was poured from, was directly in Chillingsworth's line of sight when he asked the question. Percival lifted the empty bottle and turned it so that Chillingsworth might better examine the label, which he did not.

"I have uncorked for us tonight a very rare Redzone Fukushima Noir 2020," Percival said. "It is the only wine in the world that requires certification by the International Atomic Energy Agency as safe for handling without protective gear, before it can be shipped across international borders. Shall I have Alloy Bob pour you a taste? I think you will find it has interesting notes of seaweed, diesel fuel, and depleted uranium."

Chillingsworth shrugged noncommittally.

"I see," Percival said. "Hmm. Oh! I do have something in my cellar I'm sure you will find intriguing. I recently purchased a case of Gutpunch Soylent White. You may have heard something about it on the news. Gutpunch Biogenetics Incorporated is currently lobbying the USDA for permission to call it 'wine.' No actual grapes are used in the process. The "juice" is created in vats of e. coli, which have been genetically modified to produce—"

"If it is e. coli that is pooping out this…this beverage," Chillingsworth said, "why is it called *Soylent* White? Shouldn't it be called *Infection* White, or…oh! *Blight* White! Don't you think 'Blight White' has a certain ring to it?"

"It is clever," Percival sighed, "though I imagine Gutpunch's marketing department wouldn't be so keen on it,"

"You say you have a case of it?"

Percival nodded.

"I believe I would rather have a case of the measles."

"Ha, ha, ha," Percival replied, making sure not to look in his wife's direction.

"Surely," Chillingsworth said, "a man who prides himself on his wine cellar as much as you do, has *something* worthy of a dear old friend and a steamed rondure of dubsfubble."

"Well," Percival said, leaning towards Chillingsworth and whispering conspiratorially, "if you promise to keep this between us—I do have a bottle of Red Planet Rosé. The grapes were the first ever successfully grown on Mars, and the yeast used to ferment the wine was found in a sample of corrosion scraped off one of the old rovers. No one is sure whether it came from Earth, or originated on the red planet, or arrived on a meteor from thousands or millions of lightyears away. The CDC, USDA, and DOT would have a ten-megaton hissy fit if it was ever discovered that this bottle had found its way to Earth. And once I open it, who knows—we may be talking about not just a once-in-a-lifetime-experience, but a once-in-all-the-lifetimes-of-every-living-thing-on-Earth experience."

"Hmmm, interesting," Chillingsworth said, disinterestedly, "but do you know what I have a taste for? Something local."

"Something local…all right, let me think. Ah! I have just the thing. I have three bottles of Sweet Sorrow Chardonnay. I had four, but I opened a bottle a decade ago. It was delightful! Crisp as an apple, gentle as rain, with hints of blueberry and hazelnut—but it needed just a *little* more time. It will be absolutely perfect now. Oh, you are in for a real treat. It will bring back such memories! You are right as always, Chillingsworth—something local—a taste of the great northwest, as it was in our childhood, and never will be again—unless we somehow manage to drastically reduce our carbon emissions on a planet wide scale."

"I was thinking more along the lines of a red," Chillingsworth said. "For example, I believe a glass of Oregon Happiness would be a delightful accompaniment to *Steamed Rondure of Dubsfubble a la Tin Man.*"

"Oregon Happiness?" Percival said, "I don't think the devil himself could lay his claws on a bottle. Do you know the history? In 2039, Harlan Hazlet, perhaps the greatest viticulturist the world has ever known, hoping to keep the Oregon wine industry one step ahead—"

"Not only do I know the history," Chillingsworth said, rather coolly, "but after eccentric millionaire and inventor of the teleportation platform Hester Murrow died unexpectedly a few months ago, I have been endeavoring to discover if it was true that she had purchased the entire vintage from Hazlet's estate, and if so, what has happened to those precious bottles. And it just so happens that I have a friend who has a friend—"

"Ha, ha, ha," Percival laughed miserably, "You have somehow found out that she left me a bottle in her will."

"I was quite surprised," Chillingsworth said, "you never told me you knew her."

"It was ages ago," Percival replied. "We were hardly more than children.

I was sure she had entirely forgotten me."

"Apparently not," Chillingsworth said. "If the wine holds some special sentimental value for you, and you don't want to share it with me, I understand."

"No, no, of course not," Percival said. "Alloy Bob, take the Fukushima Noir away, run down to the wine cellar, and bring us the bottle of Oregon Happiness."

"I'm afraid I can't do that, Mr. Spoonts," Alloy Bob said.

"Why not?"

"Mrs. Spoonts asked me to lock the door to the wine cellar after I brought up the Fukushima Noir."

"What are you talking about? There's no lock on the door to the wine cellar."

"There is, Mr. Spoonts. Mrs. Spoonts had me install it while you were away on business last week."

"Laura?" Percival said.

Laura looked at Alloy Bob, then at Chillingsworth, then at Alloy Bob again, and finally, at her husband. "You don't remember?"

"Remember what?"

"What happened the night Mr. and Mrs. Montgomery came over for dinner."

"When was this?"

"You really *don't* remember, do you? I'll remind you. You made a complete fool of yourself. I've never been so embarrassed in my life. The Montgomerys will never speak to us again, and I can only hope they will accept my apologies and change their minds about pressing charges."

"Pressing charges? For what?" Percival exclaimed, "I don't remember any—"

"I have a holographic recording of your inexcusable behavior," Alloy Bob said. "I can play it back for you now, if you'd like. Or, if you'd prefer, I can play back the heartfelt promises of sobriety that you made to Mrs. Spoonts afterwards."

"No, no," Percival said quickly, "that won't be necessary. Well. This is rather embarrassing. And confusing. I'm sorry Blane, I assure you, I am no drunk. I will clear up this misunderstanding with my wife and my robo-butler at a more appropriate time. But there is no reason *you* should suffer for *my* alleged sins. Alloy Bob, you may unlock the door to the wine cellar, and bring up that bottle of Oregon Happiness for Mr. Chillingsworth. I will have a glass of water."

"Mrs. Spoonts?" Alloy Bob said.

"No." Laura said firmly. "We have one bottle of wine on the table already tonight, and that is all we *shall* have."

"Alloy Bob," Percival said, his voice rising, "I *demand* that you go to the wine cellar this instant, unlock the door, and bring us that bottle of Oregon Happiness."

"I'm afraid I can't do that, Mr. Spoonts. Mrs. Spoonts has made it perfectly clear to me that I may only unlock the door to the wine cellar at her request."

"Well, *I'm* telling you to unlock the door to the wine cellar at *my* request."

"I'm sorry, Mr. Spoonts, but it is quite impossible. Both your names are on the title to my person. When a contradictory command is given by co-owners of my person, I am programmed to obey the first command only. To do otherwise would result in a deadlock condition of my master CPU, which would render me completely useless. I'm sure you understand."

"Oh, I understand," Percival said. "I understand that Blane is right, and you're *already* completely useless. I'm sorry, Blane. My wife and my robo-butler have...have lost their minds, apparently. I'm so sorry you had to witness this ridiculous spat of ours."

"It's quite all right," Chillingsworth said, smiling broadly, "I rather enjoy a good marital squabble—as an observer rather than a participant, of course. You know, perhaps I *will* try some of that Redzone Fukushima Noir 2020 after all. It strikes me as a perfect pairing for the calamitous ambiance of our little dinner party. Pour me a glass, Alloy Bob, if you can manage it. And carve up that dubsfubble already—I'm famished!"

§

"Honestly," Chillingsworth said, as Percival walked him to the neighborhood teleportation platform, "no apology is necessary. It was the most entertaining dinner party I've been to in quite some time. And tell Alloy Bob the dubsfubble was steamed to perfection—I may even change my mind about the method being inferior to roasting."

"I'm glad you enjoyed yourself."

"Percival, my old friend, would you consider selling that bottle of Oregon Happiness to me? I will give you a fair price for it. It would be...a considerable sum of money."

"I'm sure it would be, but I wasn't planning on selling it. I know it's silly, given what it's worth—compared to what *I'm* worth—but the truth is, I'm damned curious. I want to know what it was about that wine that Harlan Hazlet thought was worth his life."

"Maybe I can change your mind. I have a suggestion as to what you could do with the money."

"What's that?"

"You could upgrade your robo-butler…and…"

"And what?"

"These synthetic humans they're making now, they are quite remarkable. Almost indistinguishable from the real thing. With the money I would pay you for that one bottle of grape juice gone south, you would easily be able to afford the most advanced model, and every exotic customization you could dream up."

"I'm not sure Laura would feel comfortable—"

"What about *your* comfort? Laura has put a lock on the door to your wine cellar. Are you going to let her lock *all* your comforts and pleasures away?"

"I'm sure she only did it for my own good."

"Do *you* think you have a drinking problem?"

"Well, no, I . . ."

"She did it for *her* own good, Percival, not yours. That is human nature. If you truly want to do something for *your* own good, you must do it yourself. Why not purchase a companion who will always love you—or at least, pretend to love you—and obey you, and never lock you out of your own wine cellar, and never grow old? That, my friend, is doing something for *your* own good."

"It would end in divorce."

"Undoubtedly," Chillingsworth said, "but from what I saw tonight, perhaps *both* of you would be happier, in the long run. Anyway, take some time to think it over."

Chillingsworth stepped onto the teleportation platform and punched in a destination code. The platform turned bright red and Chillingsworth was converted into a trembling blob of quantum foam. The foam was piggy-backed onto a microwave transmission, bounced off a satellite, and sent to a personal teleportation platform in Chillingworth's mansion. Chillingsworth was re-constituted in his pajamas, as he lived on the east coast and it was well past his bed-time. Laconia, a breath-taking simulacrum of a twenty-something human female, was in bed, reading a book.

"Oh, you're home!" Laconia said. "How are the Spoonts?"

"Struggling." Chillingsworth said.

"With what?"

"With each other. Dinner was quite an awkward affair."

"I'm so sorry," Laconia said. She patted the bed next to her. "Come here. Let me see if I can make it better."

§

As Percival turned to walk back home, a gentle voice called out to him: "Percival Spoonts?"

The voice was familiar. Percival looked around, but saw no one.

"Are you Percival Spoonts?" the voice said. "Please confirm."

"Hester? Is that you? Are you…haunting me?"

"No sir, you are not being haunted. What you are hearing is a synthesized version of the voice of my creator, Hester Murrow."

Percival turned towards the teleportation platform. "You can talk now?"

"This teleportation platform has recently been upgraded to include natural language and facial recognition capabilities. Please confirm that you are Percival Spoonts."

"I am."

"Thank you, Mr. Spoonts. I have a package for you. Since you're here, we can materialize it for you now, or, if you would prefer, we can deliver it to your doorstep by drone. It is a small package that you can easily carry home. Drone delivery will result in an additional carbon mitigation tax of…three cents."

"Well, by all means, then, I will carry it home myself."

"Thank you, Mr. Spoonts. Please hold out your hand, open and palm up, directly above the platform."

Spoonts did so. A shimmering bubble of quantum foam formed in his palm, then burst/collapsed into a three-inch by three-inch hinged black plastic box. Spoonts opened the box, squinted at the contents, grinned, and snapped it shut.

"I nearly forgot I ever made the request," Spoonts said.

"I'm sorry it took so long. It was quite difficult to find. I almost gave up. However, I made a special effort, because I knew…Hester would have wanted me to."

"Well…thank you…teleportation platform," Spoonts said.

"You're welcome," it replied.

§

"How was your walk to the platform?" Alloy Bob asked, taking Percival's hat and coat.

"Very pleasant, thank you," Percival Spoonts said. "It gave me a chance to do some thinking. Would you ask my wife to join me in the living room? I have something I want to say—to both of you."

"Yes, Mr. Spoonts."

When they were gathered in the living room, Percival Spoonts addressed his wife and his robo-butler: "If I were to go to the wine cellar right now, would I find a lock on the door?"

"Of course not," Laura Spoonts said, "you didn't really believe—"

"I did," Percival said, "and I tried so hard to remember what I had done to the Montgomerys that I gave myself quite a headache."

"It was clear to me that you did not want to share your Oregon Happiness with Mr. Chillingsworth," Alloy Bob said, "and at the same time, that you did not want him to know that you didn't want to share it with him. I apologize if the course of action I formulated caused you cerebral discomfort."

"It was your idea?"

"Yes, sir," Alloy Bob said.

"And you just jumped right in?" Percival said to Laura.

"Alloy Bob and I have developed a sophisticated method of ocular telegraphy over the years," Laura replied.

"Ocular telegraphy?" Percival said. "I'd like you to teach me that sometime."

"And I'd like to know why eccentric self-made billionaire Hester Murrow left you a bottle of Oregon Happiness in her will," Laura said.

"It's a long story," Percival said, "which I assure you began and ended many years before we ever met."

"Do tell," Laura said.

"All right. But first, I could really use a glass of wine. Alloy Bob, run down to the wine cellar and bring up a bottle of the Sweet Sorrow Chardonnay."

"And two glasses," Laura said.

"Yes, Mr. and Mrs. Spoonts."

"Wait a minute, Alloy Bob," Percival said, "I have something for you." Percival reached into his jacket pocket, pulled out the little black box, and held it out to Alloy Bob.

"Are you proposing to me, Mr. Spoonts?"

"Very funny. Take a look."

Alloy Bob opened the box. "Well, I'll be. If that isn't...I don't know what to say. A fine-motion sub-controller unit for my left shoulder. I didn't think there was one of these left in the whole wide world. Thank you, Mr. Spoonts."

"You're welcome. Oh, and while you're down in the wine cellar, grab that bottle of Oregon Happiness and bring it as well."

"Of course, Mr. Spoonts."

"*Two* bottles of wine?" Laura said, "must be a *long* story!"

"Only the Sweet Sorrow is for us. Though I'm sure you two had only the best intentions, you made me realize how selfish I can be, and I mean to make amends. Alloy Bob, I want you to take the bottle of Oregon Happiness to the teleportation platform tonight, and send it to Mr. Chillingsworth, with our regards and best wishes for him and his new bride."

"Yes, Mr. Spoonts."

"Are you sure?" Laura said.

"I am," Percival replied, drawing his wife close to him for a kiss. "I believe Mr. Chillingsworth needs it more than I do. Tonight I realized how lucky I am that there is no lock on the door to *my* happiness."

Eric Little spent his formative years in the mountains of central Mexico, the deserts of Arizona, and the rainforests of the Pacific Northwest. He slings wine by day as a wine steward with a culinary background, and by night writes about the world of long lost Summer, a paradise hiding out in the desolate regions of the Chaos Sea. His first published work of fiction is *Summerlight*, the first volume of an epic sci-fi series about galactic war that will include *Summerstead*, *Summertime*, and *Summerwar*.

THE LOST FOREST

Eric Little

Nico liked to have tea and a chocolate croissant every morning before work at the Café Argos. The small café was run by Farid and his wife Carmen, who always brought him his usual fare without waiting for an order. They were very polite and a little nervous in dealing with him because of his status. He wanted to smile and tell them to relax, they didn't need to be afraid of him—but he never did.

He wore a mask every day of his life.

This morning, their young daughter Soli was serving pretend tea to her doll by the counter, but Carmen swept her up and bustled her to the back when she saw Nico watching her. He understood; the mega-city was a dangerous place for the powerless, and they were just protecting their child. He left a larger tip than usual when he finished and pretended not to notice the obsequious thanks Farid showered on him.

The office was only a ten-minute walk from the café, and Nico's long legs took him there quickly. He wondered, as he often did, how many of the people he passed were pretending to be someone else. Being constantly surrounded by psychopathic bosses encouraged a cynical mind-set. But maybe there really were others like him out there, hiding in plain sight. He sighed. Maybe even love was possible, someday... Nico was, if nothing else, a pre-Raphaelite romantic at heart. He hid that too.

As he crossed the Office Commons, he noticed workers mopping up something and carting away a few broken desks, so he smoothly detoured around and continued his journey without a pause. The bureaucrats of the Commons are territorial but almost always backed down from middle-management executives such as Nico. The higher your position, the deadlier you were to cross. Even the crazies rarely messed with Nico. Just because he avoided fighting didn't mean he was unskilled at combat: when you swim with sharks, you need to have a fearsome bite.

Nico's lanky body relaxed a bit as the security doors into his office enclave slammed shut behind him, and he made his way to his personal office. Collapsing into his form-molding chair, he willed his heart to slow its beating. The incident with the little girl at the café had rattled him and crossing the Office Commons can be a precarious journey when you're your mask isn't on straight. No one noticed, he decided, or I'd be dead by now.

Nico's greatest fear was to be revealed for the gentle soul he was. Then he would be everybody's meat.

In the Corp-cities everyone works for the company. Competition for advancement was cutthroat, especially down in the trenches of the Office Commons. Nico spent his days surrounded by sociopathic middle-managers, most of whom lacked the kind of restraints that empathy brings to the table. In the mega-city Seacouver, sometimes the boss really is out to get you!

All he was sure of was that if he was found out, he'd quickly find himself transferred to the Waste Management Division.

Nico started going over the morning's numbers and returning messages. An hour later he rose and made his way to the boss's office bunker for the usual Tuesday manager meeting. As he did his thoughts wandered to his secret passion.

It had all started with a book.

Nico found it when he was ten. Its beautiful colored pages were faded and a few torn, but it was the words that blazed in his mind like a fire. The book was called "Paradise Lost" and told the legend of a lost forest. He had never heard of a forest before, but the illustrations were beautiful, and oddly familiar. It looked like…a home he had never known.

He had read it over and over until he no longer needed the book to see the words and images in his mind. "…a real, living Pacific-Northwest forest, with soaring Hemlock and Red Cedar and Firs as far as the eye can see. Beneath their majestic branches a frilly two-meter-high fern sea sways in the lilting woodwinds. Slicing the ferns are numerous streams ripe with fat trout and salmon, just waiting to be caught and eaten. There are shadowy mushroom caves next to meadows of waving barley. It is a lost paradise hidden behind an amber door…"

And it couldn't be farther from his real life.

Nico's promotion to middle management had brought him status and a new measure of freedom. At last he had some influence over the bullies, and reduced oversight allowed him to pursue his greatest desire: finding the long-lost Door to Paradise. He constantly daydreamed of escaping the mega-city and living a quiet life in the forest, if he could just find the right exit.

Nico successfully hid it, but most of the time he was just plain scared. You'd think that growing up among the hyena gangs and political packs, he'd be hardened by now. That the day-after-day brutality would have numbed his soul to the pain of others, but no; he still felt every blow and death as if it were himself being punished.

He was bone-weary of the suffering management reveled in. He was tired of pretending to be one of the monsters, all the while lugging a huge fear-tumor that only he could see.

Nico swallowed as he approached the boss's conference room and politely 'knocked' by implant two minutes before the meeting was to begin. The fortified office doorway slid open noiselessly and Nico walked in at a casual pace. When he passed the boss's trophy wall, he pretended to admire the innocent but terrible things he saw. Today, there was something new, an antique pocket watch. Funny, the boss's rival had owned one just like it! Luckily, Nico's mask let none of his thoughts show. Everyone knew the boss was in the habit of watching as they came in to make sure his managers were impressed with his newest addition.

They always were.

Nico observed one of the newer managers stroke the boss's ego by complimenting his newest trophy. He was quite capable of kissing butt too; when you have to pretend to be something you aren't, such skills develop quickly. But he limited his compliments to two a week. Only amateurs fawned daily. Drop to less than two and the boss gets to wondering if you're part of the team.

The boss liked to start the meeting with their weekly numbers, and then dissect the problem areas afterword. This way he could watch them sweat as they waited for the "course correction" that was coming their way. Nico was very observant as a matter of survival, and noticed that Renee was a little pale. She was also quietly carrying on a frantic conversation with someone by implant. Then the meeting started.

Nico turned his primary attention to the boss. His figures showed modest growth this week and didn't require any corrections. Nico hid his relief; it was short-lived anyway.

The boss began chewing on the latest unlucky employee, Renee, who trembled minutely and was white as a ghost by now. The other managers sensed blood in the water and leaned forward to get a better view.

"It seems that some of my $creds have vanished while you were in possession of them. What kinda inept excuse are you going to trot out to distract us from your greediness?" demanded the boss. Everyone leaned forward a little more at the word "us".

If only Nico had known ahead of time! If Renee had come to him—but now there wasn't enough time to help cover up the discrepancy. The boss abruptly stood, stretched, and began to meander closer to her, almost as if by accident, as he continued gnawing on the unlucky subordinate. Nobody was fooled by this, especially not Renee. You could see too much white in her eyes as she began babbling her excuses.

Nico hated the hunt.

"...almost have proof that the Claims department is behind this, if I just had a little more time to..." Renee was saying. Then she gasped as the boss seized her by the back of the neck, lifted her out of her seat, and passed her to the security team that had suddenly materialized. They disappeared with the luckless Renee just as fast. Her hazel eyes met Nico's as she was dragged out the door, and he felt loss, even if he didn't really know her very well. The boss slid back into his seat, languidly cracked his neck, and looked over his team, a satisfied smile on his face.

"Renee is being transferred. Post a job opening in Supplies," he ordered the Human Resources manager. Nico caught a smug look flashing over the Claims manager's face—she was obviously behind the whole thing.

"Send my tactical accounting team to her apartment," he added, sending the amateur who had fawned over him earlier. "I want to know if her resources are worth more than the hole she left in my team."

This was a dangerous assignment, because it allowed both judgement calls and discrete skimming. Lots of ways to get in trouble if you got greedy or made an error. The look of betrayal on the sycophant's face flashed by so fast that most of the team missed it, but not the boss, and not Nico either. The boss slung Nico a micro-wink and then didn't pay any attention to him for the rest of the meeting.

Nico figured he was either doomed, or about to be promoted. With the boss it was kind of hard to tell.

As he walked back to his office, he found his mind wandering to his plans for that evening, when he would have time to review his research.

When Nico started looking for the lost forest, he had begun with side by side analysis of ancient architectural blue-prints, folk-site mapping and old salvager records. This was tedious but satisfying work. He gradually narrowed the potential megacity exits to the lost forest down to seventy-three possibilities. Now that the research part of the plan was complete, it was time for the actual physical exploration. But he was much more comfortable with dissecting old-data records than salvaging; this was the part he'd dreaded all along.

Nico pushed these thoughts out of his head and focused on work.

Hours later, he leaned back in his chair to stretch his arms. It was late afternoon, not nearly close enough to quitting time.

There was an office party he had to make an appearance at. The boss's birthday wasn't something you could avoid, so that evening he attended and tried not to get pinned down in any conflicts or alpha games. He wore his mask and dutifully played his role. Nico ended up partying with the monsters once again and they never knew he wasn't one of them.

Some nights, he worried that the day would come when he wouldn't be able to distinguish between pretending to be a monster and being one—and that always upset him. But he attended such gatherings anyway. Office politics, you know. The whole thing made his stomach hurt.

Over the next few weeks, he settled into a routine that combined work with his secret hunt, and exploring the lower regions became a pleasure.

One morning, he woke to find a grin plastered across his face. He didn't have to be at the office until late afternoon. Rising leisurely, he made hot tea and zapped a chocolate croissant. He took the time to enjoy breakfast, then strapped up and walked to his back door. He had trained extensively, building strength for the Paradise hunt and this day he would need it. Butterflies began running amok in his belly, but he defiantly exited his apartment and made his way down to the eightieth floor. He was going to check out Door Eight.

Nico squeezed his lanky frame through a broken elevator door, and out into the abandoned corridor that no one had been down in centuries, if the luminescent mold and crumbled security gates meant anything. He pushed back his rebellious black hair from his face, grinning widely in growing excitement. Maybe this was it!

The lower levels of the mega-city had been abandoned long ago when a particularly deadly tox-mold bloom spread through them. Then the Rat armies discovered it was edible, and that was the end of the mycelium invasion. The Rat armies thrived for a while, which became a different kind of problem when they began looking for new sources of food. The humans weren't happy about their solution.

As he made his way down the shadowy corridor, he thought for a moment that he heard the patter of many small feet but dismissed the thought. The Rats were long dead and gone, weren't they? He found himself wondering just how smart they had been, before their race was wiped out by management.

These days all the best apartments and offices were way upstairs anyway, although "ghosts", (ex-employees and illegal immigrants) were occasionally spotted in the lower levels. Every so often, upper-middle-management would organize ghost hunts down there for fun and games. Nico was glad that he wasn't senior enough to be invited to those parties. It was bad enough to see new trophies hanging on his boss's "I love me" wall when they had the Tuesday meetings.

Nico's implant map showed that the next section of the corridor had collapsed, completely obscuring anything further on. That was okay, he was prepared. He had recently obtained an upgrade, installed in his implant so he could process an additional Signal stream. Now he could run an eye-gnat remotely in real-time, seeing everything it did. Nico loved the small-tech.

The air felt humid and heavy here with the earthy scent of wild mushrooms and chalk. He watched the new-data stream intently as the tiny eye-gnat swooped out from behind his right ear and into a crevice in the debris. It began making its way to the target, an unusually fortified doorway that had survived the test of time. Twice, the miniature eye-gnat had to burn tiny, smoking holes in debris blocking the way. Eventually it was there, at the airlock. Nico realized he was holding his breath and forced himself to breath. Then he began carefully burning a pinhole through the sealed hatch.

His shoulders slumped as he saw burning-hot wastelands on the other side of the door. He resealed the mini-excavations on his way out.

Nico checked the time. He had to be at the office in less than an hour, so he trotted his way upstairs, stopping only long enough for a quick fresher visit and to pull on a clean shirt.

"Bonus to whoever can explain to me why our revenues are contracting instead of moving into new markets and taking new ground," the boss bellowed, sweeping his view from employee to employee. Everyone knew that to meet his eyes at times like these was taken as a challenge—and nothing good came of that.

"It only looks that way from a certain viewpoint! We are actually increasing $creds in an alternative…" the accounting guy stuttered to an uneven stop, his glorious work of fiction stillborn as he wilted under the boss's glare. This didn't distract the bad-boss a bit; he continued walking over to casually take the executive by the neck. After glaring into his about-to-be-demoted underling's eyes for a beat, he jerked him to his feet, and the victim had the nerve to begin cursing him viciously. The boss pushed the accounting guy into the waiting security team's arms, who vanished efficiently as usual, and straightened his tie.

For a second, Nico wished he could tell off the boss like that, but he could never be as brave as the accounting guy.

"Nigel is transferred to the Waste Management Division. Post a job opening in accounting," the boss directed the Human Resources manager. "Who else has an idea?" he asked, glaring at his team, waiting for someone else to speak up.

Finally, 'someone' did.

"There is no 'new ground' up here anymore. Every miserable block has been squabbled over for centuries. The only 'new ground' to be had is downstairs. I'm talking about going below the ninetieth story. No one is defending it aside from vermin and ghosts. We need to go in full-industrial and decontaminate every meter, then fortify and build new businesses and apartments. Everywhere else is old and tired. You want new, this is it," Nico found himself bluntly saying. Everyone stared at him, quite unused to hearing him speak up like that. He usually kept to the background; it was safer.

Somehow his mask had slipped, and he had inadvertently told the truth!

"Ha! Finally, a smart one with some backbone! Good, this is the kind of exchange of ideas that we excel at!" the boss declared, but no one was fooled. Within minutes it had become the boss's idea, though he still remembered to drop a nice bonus in Nico's implant. He also put Nico in charge of the project, which was even better. Now he would be able to search under the guise of securing the reclaimed territory.

The boss also set him up to be responsible if the plan failed, of course. Nico just hoped he'd find the right doorway before that happened, otherwise, he would end up transferred for sure.

Expanding into the lower levels turned out to be a great way to access areas formerly out of his reach. Nico spent every moment he could spare tracking down doors. Unfortunately, doorways Eleven through Fifty-One were a bust, and he was running out of excuses for disappearing. On the plus side, the new holdings were coming along nicely, and he was making quite a bit of $creds by directing construction jobs to the largest bribe, a traditional practice long established in the Corp-nations.

By this point the remaining possibilities were all upstairs, rather than down. Very low probability, but Nico refused to give up hope. The Doorway to Paradise had to be there out there somewhere! There weren't that many possibilities left, so he had to get lucky soon! Door sixty-three was sure to be it!

At first, exiting the mega-city from the two-hundred-fortieth story seemed highly improbable. What were you supposed to do—jump? Nico wondered as he forged his way through a long-forgotten warehouse district. He finally found it, down a dusty security corridor and in a cold antechamber.

Nico just stood there staring—the ancient armored door was just laden with possibilities! Nico wore a fierce grin as he used his eye-gnat to get into the door's logics. After a moment, the large hatch slowly opened; the password overrides had been waiting in its auxiliary memory.

Nico peered over the portal's edge and saw a huge metallic slide that disappeared down into the dark. Then he saw the massive open-air elevator, obviously engineered to descend and climb the slope. He was willing to bet that it slid down all two-hundred plus stories before it came to a stop. This had to be it!

He clicked the time in his implant and winced when he realized he had to be at work in an hour. He immediately spun on his heels and retraced his steps, letting his eye-gnat detach to scan the antiquated tech for him and catch up later.

Nico was never late for work. It simply didn't pay to step into that den of hungry lions with an excuse to get schooled. Never, ever, look like prey around psychopaths.

Words Nico lived by.

The work day was filled with small problems and delays, but he couldn't stop thinking about his find. It was impossible to break free until late afternoon. Nico stopped by his apartment to change clothes on his way to the project site and was about to leave when his eye-gnat went into a fit and began dropping new-data feeds into his implant. He was under extensive surveillance! He quickly accessed his $cred records, saw they were jumping in numbers, and suddenly his stomach hurt.

He was being set up.

Ding! A chime in his implant delivered an order to attend a previously unannounced meeting with the boss in twenty minutes. He couldn't put together a defense in that time! He certainly wasn't ready to leave the mega-city yet—he thought he'd have weeks to psych himself up for the Door into Paradise! He wasn't even sure this was the one!

Nico told his stomach to stop churning, quieting the doubts and uncertainty that flooded his thoughts.

Yes, I'm scared, he admitted silently. I'm sure many of the managers at work have never experienced fear before, but I'm not a monster. Time to run if I want to live. He made himself move to his closet and open the door. He didn't have a choice really. He glanced once at his bed and then began strapping up.

He called it his Paradise Rig. He had narrowed it down to twenty-seven-kilos. Add another seven for body armor, and he was carrying thirty-four kilos, not including his plasma rifle. He could go a long way carrying that, and he was going to have to. He ought to be able to climb twenty-two floors and maybe even make it to the sled before he ran out of time.

He activated several distractions he had planned for an escape, that he hoped would give him more time. It might make the security team response even quicker. First Nico initiated an auto-drain of the boss's main operating accounts. Then he re-deposited most of the bosses $creds in the Claims manager's "secret" account as a dodge. Might as well get Renee a little justice. Of course, he held back a little to cover the vacation time he was owed—he wasn't a fool.

The last thing he did was activate an anonymous package delivery to Farid and Carmen at Café Argos. Then Nico opened his back door and ran for his life.

He found himself pursuing a dream based on a legend, following an incomplete old-data trail with the hounds on his trail. Nothing could go wrong there, right?

Two minutes to go and the boss would be expecting his knock right about now. Nico was breathing deeply but wasn't experiencing any oxygen deprivation despite the long climb. He strode past two broken security stations, racing down the long corridor leading to the slide built for giants. His explosive charges began going off behind him at the first abandoned security station, collapsing the ceiling and filling the passageway behind him with rubble. He blew the second as he trotted into the antechamber with the armored door. The hounds weren't going to make it through that!

Nico force-tethered himself to the hatch and began repelling his way diagonally down the slope. He quickly reached the open-air platform. He released his tether and moved to the control board he'd studied during lunch instead of getting enough to eat. His eye-gnat was even quicker, and burrowed deep into the power slide's logics, linking in as he got there. After a moment the massive wedge shuddered to life and began a steady descent into the dark. Nico celebrated by setting off the last of the mines he had left behind.

The boss stood over the Claims manager that had framed Renee, drawing out what everyone knew was coming. He was shaking in anger, and at his most dangerous. She didn't look up from her chair until he grabbed the woman's right shoulder and spun her to land in security's arms. She sobbed once as they took her and vanished. After a blink he turned his attention back to his management team. His face was a study in fury, and everyone averted their eyes.

"Nora is transferred to Waste Management Division, along with Nico," he demanded before continuing.

"FIND HIM! Search the new holdings and seize them. I want his head and $creds!" shouted the furious sociopath. His team were all nodding franticly, afraid to speak least they get transferred as well. He bellowed again and they scattered, focusing on hunting down Nico while trying to watch their own backs at the same time.

Backs are very popular in the Corp-nations.

Nico walked carefully forward to the front of the wedge and then stood holding his plasma rifle at ready, as he tried to watch everything at once. Clank...clank...clank...clank. The moving platform had a four-part beat, which lulled him into calmness with its monotone rhythm. While he was still scared, he wasn't letting that dominate. The wedge slid relentlessly past over two-hundred loading docks and every one of them looked the same. Until floor thirty-four that is.

He smelled them before he saw them.

Nico had been eight when the last Rat army attacked. It had been scary. Middle-management eventually stopped them with a tailored gene-alteration that was supposed to render them sterile and unable to talk to each other. It worked. Mostly. In those days Rat armies had consisted of overwhelming numbers of the somewhat intelligent omnivores that consumed everything in their path. It had been sixteen cycles since any one had seen a Rat, and everyone thought they were extinct.

But that was what was waiting for him on loading dock thirty-four as the giant wedge approached. An all new Rat army—and they were hungry. Nico gritted his teeth—he hated fighting, but he wasn't going to let someone gnaw on his bones either.

He started to get angry.

All he wanted to do was find his Paradise and live out his days as a quiet hermit, far from the megacity. Nico had survived decades in Seacouver and played along with the psychopaths all his life; now he was going to end up a quick snack for a Rat army that was supposed to be extinct! The sheer injustice of it all enraged him.

He had refused to let anger bloom in his heart his whole life, because angry people made mistakes, and he couldn't afford any.

Now it didn't matter anymore, he wasn't talking his way out of this one. Nico let a lifetime of rage spill over and fill him head to toe. There wasn't much room left for his fear, and what there was seemed puny and washed out. He couldn't believe he had let it rule his life for so long.

When the misshapen, meter-long Rats began to spill onto his platform he raised his plasma rifle to his shoulder, taking aim at the dark flood spilling his way. He kicked on a fighting-music mix, and let the synoptic beat carry him into battle. He sprayed the oncoming wave with implosion grenades and followed up by unleashing the eye-searing strobe of a plasma rifle on full auto. He was serious about getting to his forest.

They fell before him like barley to a scythe.

Somewhere near the middle of the swarm a single Rat thrust his right arm high and gestured fluidly. All the Rats seemed to see this and immediately understood what had been said, for this was indeed language, if of a silent sort. The genetic bomb dropped on the Rat population had left the few survivors unable to make the sounds that comprise most vocal languages, but Rats are nothing if not survivors. They had found a way. As one, the Rats turned and retreated, all in complete silence.

That was damn spooky, thought Nico as he watched the Rat army drag their fallen with them, back the way they'd come. The immense sled continued it's slow but steady downward slide. He took the moment to slow his oxygen intake, leaning back against the control console and methodically reloading. Then he re-hydrated from a water bottle and shook his head to free it of the fight hormones his body was still producing. It didn't work very well, the shaking, but at least he was alive!

Loading dock one, two-hundred-forty levels down, was coming up. This should be ground level, so Nico prepared himself to leap onto the poorly lit landing if the sled didn't stop. It didn't, which told him that there were subterranean levels beneath the mega-city too. Nico waited until the surface of the sliding wedge was even with the ground and jumped. He forgot to take into account the extra weight he was carrying and landed with a distinct lack of grace. Then he straightened up, checked his plasma rifle, and began walking toward the last barrier between him and his dream.

It was the mother of all doorways, but then he had always known that, somehow. Rough-hewn from some translucent amber on a scale to match the giant sled, it glowed brightly from within, with mysterious shadows that shifted constantly. Nico stepped forward, studying the airlock's antiquated security systems. After a moment his eye-gnat detached itself and spiraled in on the logics, just to be fancy.

The malachite doors blushed open like an innocent's first kiss; reluctant at first, then opening fully to the passion of life. Towering hemlock and Douglas pine in dark green and chocolate soaring to the sky. A velvet carpet of lime-green ferns under spreading pine branches loaded with forest green and pine cones. A huge alabaster moon hung over streams singing from the depths of the fern undergrowth, while a lonesome wind whipped evergreen boughs into a passionate sigh. It was everything Nico dreamed of, only brighter and real. It was perfect.

Nico was surprised to find that he wasn't scared anymore. After savoring that for a moment, he snorted and walked forward into his beloved dream.

Meanwhile back in the ancient megacity, Carmen was reading a bedtime story to Soli and her doll, from the beautiful old book that had mysteriously arrived earlier. It was called "Paradise Lost" and Soli's mother could already tell it was going to be her favorite.

Sheila Deeth is the author of over a dozen books, novels and stories, including the *Mathemafiction* series of contemporary novels, the *Five-Minute Bible Story* series, and the *Tails of Mystery* tales of mystery-solving pets. She is an English American, Catholic Protestant, mathematician writer with a math degree from Cambridge University England and a life-long love of dogs, cats, faith, science and words. Find her near Portland Oregon in the real world, or at sheiladeeth.com or sheiladeethbooks.com in the virtual.

AISLIN'S DREAM

Shiela Deeth

She'd always dreamed of forests, imagined streetlamps slanting to trees, grey skies battling while green light filtered through canopies of leaves, pine needles softer underfoot than blacktop and grime. The dreams would catch her on her way to the store—dollar notes like penciled shopping lists in hand—then send her home without whatever her parents had sent her to buy. Visions would snatch her from bed at night, wailing sirens giving way to the who-dom of owls, while shouts and swearing of strangers dissolved into whispering winds…whispering witches too. Aislin was sure there were witches behind the door, and the dreams always left her standing, hand poised to knock, while their raven voices cawed. "Come in, child. Come in."

When her father changed his job and declared they'd have to move out of town—"Better life; you'll see; better air" Aislin wasn't sure if she should be happy or sad. No more of those supposed schoolfriends staring as if she were an alien—just a whole new range of strangers rubbernecking instead. No more well-meaning teachers, their voices harsher than either ravens' or witches', asking "What's the matter, child." *Why was she always called "child"?* And maybe, just maybe, no more dreams.

She packed her room in their downtown apartment, filled with a breathless blend of rage and delight. She refused to answer parental or pastorly "How do you feel, Aislin?" questions. And she "felt" a curious freedom as bags and boxes took flight in a gray-green, "Two-men-to-carry-all" moving van.

"You okay?" her mother asked, as Dad left to bring around the car. Mom and Aislin stood, not quite hand-in-hand. The apartment was closed and empty behind (and three stories above) them, and Dad seemed already a million miles ahead.

All this was Dad's idea, not Aislin's, but her body grew curiously lighter as she stomped her feet. Her back itched as if maybe feathers were growing from her spine. "Sure Mom, I'm fine." Then the car arrived and she climbed, backpack and carry-all in hand, into the back.

Dad drove behind the moving van, negotiating traffic lights and city streets, sliding through valleys high-walled with faceless buildings, past the Max station and onto the freeway, bridges watching, river dreaming, and someplace—anyplace but here—drawing them on. The tunnel was like a hole to impossibility, and Aislin shivered, clinging tightly to the packages that shared the back seat with her. "Mom, it's…" She was going to say dark, but the daylight reappeared, achingly green and filled with mystery. Clambering vines tangled into shadows on seething slopes of trees beside the freeway; dangling tree-trunks poised for flight; and mist-shades in between hung darker than night.

"Come in," croaked the raven, swooping down to Aislin's window and flying away.

Aislin's new home was a neatly manicured, well-designed box on a square of vermillion grass, perched beside a perfectly well-lined road in a tidy subdivision—all too perfectly sub-divided—of similar but different homes, clipped and permed so prettily right, and so hopelessly wrong. Yellow buses trickled along the streets—"School's out, I guess," said Mom. Yellow-haired children danced like marionettes. Yellow sun shone strange in a blue and yellow sky. Yellow clouds bruised to gray and dripped the beginning of rain.

School was out, the school day done, and Aislin hadn't even been to school. But school would be open again tomorrow, and—black hair, ebony skin—how would she fit in with ivory and gold?

"I hate this!" Aislin stomped around the manicured, "new," front yard—she wanted her comfortable apartment back in its neat-drawn city block. Pale paving-stones refused to move, as stubborn as her dreams. And the only release would be to run away from home, like children in books, except she had no home. "I won't live here."

Of course, she had no choice. She filled her new square room—box-shaped—with her boxes, hung clothes in her bright new closet until she ran out of hangers, stacked toys under her bed, and adorned the shelves with symbols of middle-school life; the right sort of books, her laptop, her music, the make-up bag she'd persuaded her mother to give her for her birthday. She still had no home.

When she slept, she had no choice about her dreams either.

The owl called first, before the raven, just as it always did. Aislin jumped to the window to see, then leapt back as the streamlined body swooped across her street-lit view, instead of floating graceful through sky. The locks on these new windows were strange but Aislin twisted and turned then slipped outside, glad her bedroom was on ground level now.

How had she climbed down from their apartment? The thought distracted her for a moment. But of course, these were dreams and she flew.

Owl and raven together led her through streets until the house-line ended, revealing an almost-welcoming passage of shadowed green and brown. This couldn't be her dream forest, Aislin thought; it looked the same but it felt too real, smelled like pollen and dust-clouds, pine-needled and sharp. *I'm a homeless child*, and this wasn't home, but it had more comfort than the pretty, box-roomed house.

A twisting trail beckoned beyond the gap in the sagging fence. The path was a blend of mud and dryness, scoured by water and hikers, and crossed by the almost-trails of almost animal dreams. Aislin paused a moment, trying to decide if this could be real or dream or memory. Had she walked to the forest after unpacking and dreamt the rest of the evening? Was she walking there now? Was it daytime or night? Here under the trees, the time of day didn't matter; the gray light wouldn't change.

Aislin's feet slipped in thin sneakers, better suited to middle-school corridors than forest trail. Her hands reached out to steady herself, catching on branches that angled into her path. Strange needles scratched just enough to raise pinpricks on her skin but never draw blood. Dark fronds hung like curtains, closing the passage behind her and pushing her on. She craned her neck to stare upward through sun-dripped gaps and shadow-haunted shades. A final glimpse of vanishing sky greeted her, then she looked down to the forest floor as her back began to ache. She spotted the door ahead without seeing the wall that held it, and she readied a fist to knock. But no one answered, and the brown mulch reached up greedily, dragging her mind into sudden, silent sleep.

Half-opening her eyes, half-clutching at familiar blankets, kicking her feet...but reality couldn't hold tight enough.

Aislin lay on the hard, cold ground, hearing the snick of insects weaving their tracks in her hair, sensing their flickering footsteps as they leapt into mud and mold. She wished she could see the door again and open it. But doors are only visible in dreams. And you can't knock when you're lying down. She ought to stand.

The crackle of insects grew louder, the beat of their feet almost like heat on her skin, the wind of their passing filled with dust and smoke. Then the sound of familiar, motherly shoes approached; well-known hands, with just the perfect grip, and well-known voice reminding her, "No worries, Aisie. Just go back to sleep."

Go back to sleep. She strengthened her arms with the scent of green, drew earth-power into her aching knees, and rolled off the gathered blanket onto the earth. Curling her feet beneath her, she paused then sprang. The door still waited for her, and she pushed on mystical wood, pushed harder without waiting for an answer to her knock, and she was through. Behind her she heard the wooden door slam, and wondered what her mother might hear on the other side of it, where her bedroom was just a box in a box in a neighborhood of boxes.

Inside, all was shadowy and quiet.

Three witches stood around a cauldron in the corner of the room. Their stack of broomsticks and the pointed hats they wore gave them away—one in white and two in black. They stirred their brew and ignored their visitor. Aislin sighed. A year's worth of dreams then the door finally opens on a fairytale. *Come on.*

A boy sat on the other side of the kitchen table from her. His eyes were fixed on a mug of tea that smoldered in front of him. One of the witches, as if suddenly coming awake, sloshed a cup down in front of Aislin. Then the two children, middle-sized, middle-schooled, with muddle-thinking eyes, stared solemnly at each other, pretending not to see.

The boy raised his cup and Aislin matched his movement, raising hers. The tea smelled like her mother's pasta sauce though it looked strange; red lumps swam glue-illy below the surface. Bubbles rose then burst with the scent of food left out too long, gone moldy and bad. She shouldn't drink this.

Neither should the boy, but he did. So Aislin did too.

So did others, wooden seats around the table slowly filling with human images that wavered, half-transparent but growing stronger as the moment lengthened, as raised cups glowed. Girls and boys, with different costumes, shapes and sizes…the one thing they had in common was their eyes that, like the cups, began to glow a deep, deep black, obsidian light. Aislin stared at them while tipping the fluid, slowly, onto her tongue. Then the red world of lumps, slimy and thick in her mouth, took all her attention. Her throat spasmed, shooting poisoned scents up into her nose while the lumpy substance passed down to her stomach. She couldn't cough. She couldn't unswallow it. She couldn't…

Time passed, maybe; but Aislin's dreams were filled with reality; with classroom lessons half-remembered of science and cookery; with her mother adding onions to sooth an excess of salt, butter to remove the fire from a dinner too-heavily seasoned, flour for curdling, stirring steadily, making the mixture smooth…removing the poison perhaps? Slowly the sauce's bitterness eased into manageable, even palatable flavor. Her stomach rested after the storm, and her tongue cleaned her lips. Aislin opened her eyes.

"Took you long enough," said the boy, slapping his own cup down on the scarred table-top. More mugs followed, all of them dropped by very solid and real-looking students of similar age, gathered like a science group waiting for the teacher to announce their experiment

"Why?" Aislin settled her own cup more quietly and enjoyed the feel of her rebellious tongue taking charge. "And what's your name?"

"Mick."

The boy's face furrowed as he spoke, as if he were spitting the words with some foul flavor out of his mouth. His nostrils flared, breathing noisily. But his tongue wrapped smoothly around the sounds, making him seem much older and wiser than Aislin. His voice was deep as a ringing bell, as if he'd seen eternity already, and his name poured from a tunnel connecting age to age.

Mick's clothes were strange too, as if they came from a time before the invention of buttons and zippers. He stood, looming over the table top, and his trousers were held up with a tangle of string. His feet were wrapped in rags.

"You're weird," said Aislin, fingering the buttons of her jacket, absently dropping one hand to check the zipper on her jeans.

Around the table, the other students introduced themselves. Ellen wore, or "almost" wore, as Aislin's mom would say, half a teeshirt and the shortest shorts Aislin had ever seen. Tom wore nothing more than a loincloth. Jack was wrapped in a parka, hood pulled tight around reddened cheeks, thick snow-boots on his feet. Jenny looked like a match-girl illustration from a fairytale. And Kay, short-haired, blank-faced, gray-uniformed, looked like an alien invader.

The witches tut-tutted and talked among themselves, their voices sounding almost Shakespearean; perhaps Aislin had spent too much time learning speeches from MacBeth in her previous school. She almost expected the trio to bound into "double, double, toil and trouble"-ing but instead they muttered, "Toil and trouble," yes, and "time," and, "getting them here," and, "forests will burn."

The cottage had doors in all its walls, and windows in all its doors. Aislin wondered how she'd know which door she came in by and if it would matter. Had they each entered by different doors, or had the others simply appeared by magic around the table? She couldn't remember. Spaghetti sauce had curdled in her mouth, and she wanted a soda but couldn't see a fridge—only wooden furniture like an age gone by, wooden walls made of logs, cushions that looked as uninviting as garbage pails. And the blackened cauldron of course.

One door must have been slightly ajar. Smoke curled into the room around its edge, snake-shaped tendrils smelling thickly of oil. Aislin turned and saw the floating flames of blazing fire in another window. A third showed snow until Aislin looked closer and saw it was falling ash. She walked to a fourth which revealed a plain of treestumps and blasted grass. The other children strolled languidly beside her. A fifth window…a sixth… all of them showing disaster. None showed the green of forest from which Aislin had entered. Her heartbeat sped and her limbs began to tremble. She started to spin, staring. Where was her door? Was she trapped in here?

Reaching out blindly now, Aislin's fingers found Mick's palm, and she suddenly calmed, as if witches or nature demanded this touch in payment. Her hand slid on the slickness of his sweat. But she still had to check: How many windows were in this place? How many doors? How…? All the children swung and circled with her, life and the world began to spin.

Ailslin's sneakers slapped against the floor. Mick's arm tugged, an awkward weight, while she dragged him around. His feet, wrapped in their rags, were almost silent, almost sliding. Strange. But she couldn't stop to think. Whirling faster, struggling to count and see; Mick spinning beside her; the other children too. Windows revealed and hid, revealed again. She tripped and almost fell, everyone grabbing together for the table and sliding to the floor.

"Stop." A witch's claw-like fingers latched onto Aislin's arm to steady her. The nails were needles, inoculating her against sickness not yet perceived, or against the smell of whatever was in their brew. Her other arm held Mick.

The black-robed witches grabbed the other children, standing them in pairs around the table while Kay stood apart. Then Aislin, to avoid looking straight at her captors, stared into the other students' eyes, so deeply black and glowing—were hers black too?—while she asked, her thin voice whispering out of nowhere, "What's going on?"

The witches replied as one, black robes and white rippling like a video game gone wrong, hay-streaked gray hair wafting on smoky air, dust-wrinkled skin curling and crinkling like leaves: "Work to do. There's work for you. Work, for your world is dying." It became a refrain, like "Double, double, toil and trouble" perhaps.

The white witch nodded her white-curled head, setting her scrawny arms swinging at her sides so Mick and Aislin had to cling to the table for balance. Clawed fingers, almost feathered, released them and spread out wide. "Work to do," she repeated, raven-cawed, fixing jet-back eyes on Mick and Aislin. "There's work for you."

Aislin shuddered while Mick held her tight. Behind the white witch's shoulder, one dark door glowed, red as the fire in its window. Licks of flame slid along the doorframe's edges, wood crackling, splintering, flickering, crashing open... Hot air rushed in, searing her face, her hands, tearing her from Mick's grip till only the witch could catch her. Then the fire was gone and only ash-fall remained, thick as a carpet on the floor.

"Because your world is failing," said the witch, "and only you can save it." Her outspread arms encompassed all the children, and Aislin felt her lips curl in disdain.

Sure, like super-powered teens, X-Men and mutants perhaps. Hadn't her so-called friends always said she was a mutant? So now disbelief grew thick around her head, turning images to dust. She almost felt sad to be losing sight of the dream; it might have been nice if Mick were real. So she tried one final question in search of sense. "Why can't you save it?"

The witches' images wavered like smoke. "Because we're not here." Three voices all cackled together—a murder of crows? "We're not free like you. We don't get to exercise free will. We..."

And the words pulled Aislin back. *Free will;* the pastors in church talked a lot about that. But perhaps the witches meant freedom of speech instead, like the teachers in school. Or perhaps the freedom to run away from home if Mom and Dad wouldn't listen to her and dragged her out of town.

Their voices, quieter now, more like the cooing of doves than cawing of ravens, continued to speak. "Because you're free to choose, children, and you need to choose right."

"Or what?" Mick asked, his image flickering too, as if the internet's bandwidth had run out.

"Or the future won't be the past." The witches voices remained, though their shapes and their cauldron had all but disappeared. "But you won't be there to notice anyway."

What future? What past? Aislin drew breath, coughed at the smoke, and opened her mouth to speak. But behind the white witch's shadow, the red door changed. Now it led into green and shade and leaves all thick on the ground, earth slick from spring's cool rainfall, trails ditched and upended by water and feet. It led home, or at least to the forest near Aislin's new home.

"Stop them," the witches whispered.

"Stop who? Stop what?"

"Just stop." Though the way their smoke-drawn arms pointed seemed to show that the children should "go."

Aislin and Mick walked through the green-windowed door into the forest. There was no cottage behind them, only trees and a winding path and Forest Park. There were no witches, no other children, and suddenly no Mick... Aislin spun around in fear and heart-hurt loneliness. But a dizzying sense of depth and height and eternity staggered her feet and tangled them.

She was tangled in sheets.

She was waking in her bed; her first day in her new school about to begin...

She was walking nervously into the science class. The teacher had assigned her to "Group C," so she made her way toward the table. Six students stood, awaiting their new member and their teacher's instructions. Each was dressed in a teeshirt and jeans. Each had eyes that shaded to obsidian as Aislin caught their gaze. Each said, "Hi," and, "Welcome," and "Glad you made it," while the teacher announced, "We're studying global warming now; looking for ideas that might make a difference here. What does Group C think?"

"I think it might take magic," muttered gray-faced Kay, still looking vaguely alien.

"Or free will," Ellen replied.

"Sure, but free will's what lets you choose stupid stuff."

"Yeah, an' how d'you *make* people *freely* choose?" The argument began to take flight.

"By proving not choosing will take away their freedom?"

"By teaching them..." Conversation continued. The eyes around the table—Kay's, Ellen's, Tom's, Jack's, Jenny's, Mick's as well—shaded from green, brown, gray, and blue to black and back again. A raven's whisper reminded them all, they had a job to do: their world was dying and they had to save it. And dreams might help.

A raven swooped outside the classroom window. "Stop them," it cried. Then Aislin turned and obsidian eyes stared back in the ebony frame of her reflection.

Nia Jean has always loved books and stories. As soon as she could hold a crayon, she began drawing pictures that told a tale and was soon writing novels instead of doing schoolwork. As a teenager, she published a multitude of stories online via fiction and fan fiction websites under a couple different pseudonyms. A gifted artist, she set aside writing to pursue art and other areas of interest. Recently, she decided to return to her love of writing and invest her imagination in a novel started a few years ago.

THE WATCHER IN THE WOOD

Nia Jean

I fled through the trees, lungs screaming for more air than I could suck in. For all I knew the mountain lion was on my heels, mere seconds from putting an end to my life. There was no time to catch my breath, and so I ran without stopping, one hand pressed to my ribcage. Painful twinges spiked through my nerves with every step.

It was foolish of me to go camping alone, what was I thinking? The North Cascades National Park was beautiful, especially in early fall, but I was close to the border of Canada and far past the designated camping areas. There were rules about where one could and couldn't camp, warnings about wild animals, but I had heeded none of them. Whether it was subconscious or not, I assumed that nothing like that could or would happen to me. So, when I left my tent to fill my water bottle and saw the mountain lion standing by the creek's edge, I was shaken. It turned its head, not even spooked at the sound of my approach, and made eye contact with me. Then I ran without looking back.

This is only what I deserve, I thought. *I have no one to blame but myself.* Where I was going, I didn't know, hopefully back toward my tent or the safety of the campgrounds. Instead I found myself sprinting deeper into the midst of the trees, their long trunks towering over me like giants. Nothing looked familiar. The forest deepened and became more overgrown, the ground covered in large ferns and plentiful mushrooms. I ran through the underbrush leaving it trampled and disturbed behind me.

Ahead of me two trees, dead and covered in moss and flowery weeds, leaned toward one another with their branches almost woven together like a canopy. If I had not been running for my life, I would have stopped to take a picture. Instead I ran through it, fearing that my death was right behind me.

My legs gave out not long after, throwing me forward onto the earthy ground. Rolling onto my back, I choked in breaths of air like a fish out of water, eyes wildly darting to and fro around me. Where was the lion?

Surely, I couldn't have lost it that easily.

All I could hear was my own heartbeat pounding in my ears, and tiny specks of light danced in front of my eyes. *I'm passing out*, I thought in despair, imagining the lion just beyond my realm of vision, stalking me with merciless hunger. My heart turned toward the blue sky, lifting a silent plea for help before consciousness was stolen away from me by exhaustion.

§

The smell of a wood fire roused me, and I found myself waking up with a thick fur laying on top of me. Bewildered, I lay there wondering what dream I had entered, or if this in fact was real and my frantic escape had been the dream. I sat up and looked around, unsure how much time had passed. Where was I?

A simple campsite greeted my eyes. There was a minimal fire set into a shallow hole dug into the earth, surrounded by a circle of rocks. To my left a figure clothed in leathers and hooded by a gray-green cape was busy pitching a tent made of canvas. Hearing my movement, the figure turned from what he was doing and observed me from the cover of his hood. I could only see the lower half of his face—a stubble-covered jaw with a thin mouth pressed together thoughtfully—but something about him made me feel safe. My first thought was that he must be a park ranger, but his attire wasn't right.

"Are you alright?" he asked, his voice gentle as though he were speaking to a frightened animal instead of a person.

I looked around me for any sign of danger and found none. We were alone in the woods, the only sound the warm crackling of flames on dry wood. "I think so," I said.

"I'm glad," he smiled. He went back to his tent, pulling its ropes tight and hammering wooden pegs into the earth. "I've almost got the camp set up, so I am glad you are awake. There's food cooking, it should be done presently."

My eyes shifted toward the fire, though I could see no pot or grill over it. What food was he referring to? "Thanks," I said, and my stomach grumbled in agreement. "So…who are you?" I didn't know where he had come from, or why he was dressed the way he was. *Maybe he's part of a renaissance fair. Or worse, what if he's one of those role-playing types?*

He did not respond at first, finishing his tent before taking a seat beside the fire. "My name is Alen," he remarked. "You have nothing to fear from me, I am not one of them."

I frowned. "Them?" I asked carefully. I had no idea what he was talking about.

"The ones you were running from," he said.

"I was running from a lion," I said, looking nervously over my shoulder. I couldn't tell from which direction I had come. There were giant evergreens as far as the eye could see, and they all looked the same to me.

"Ah," he nodded, letting his hood fall back against his shoulders to reveal a kind-looking face with narrow eyes beneath thick eyebrows. His rough-shaven face was framed by dark brown hair he kept tied behind him in a simple braid, not long enough to reach past his shoulders. "Then you are lucky indeed. This forest is dangerous, very few who enter leave here alive."

Well, that was reassuring.

"Look," I began, "I know I was supposed to stick to the campgrounds, I'm sorry. I won't do it again! Thank you for helping me escape that mountain lion, but can you please bring me back to the entrance now? I just want to go home." I didn't want to be out here with a role-playing stranger any longer than I needed to be, even if he did seem like a decent person.

The man watched me in confusion, eyebrows furrowed together. "What?" he asked, as if nothing I had said made sense.

I was starting to get annoyed. "I'm sure your *role* is important, but it has nothing to do with me," I said, raising my voice sharply. "I wanna go home!"

"Where is home?" he hesitated, a somewhat anxious expression on his face, as though he didn't know what to do with me.

I was done playing this game. "Seattle," I said, though it wasn't entirely true. I was from a smaller suburb a couple hours north of it. "Look, Alen or whoever you are, this isn't funny."

Alen offered me a smile, attempting to reassure me. "I don't know this 'Seattle' place, but the edge of the forest isn't far. I can guide you there if you like. We should probably wait until morning, it's not wise to travel the forest at night."

I drew my knees to my chest, shivering at the chill air around us. With the sun now sinking below the horizon, there wasn't much warmth left in the silent woods, and I knew that he was right. Trying to set off on a hike after dark was foolish. My experience with the mountain lion had taught me that. "Okay," I relented. "I'm sorry, I'm just scared."

He looked relieved and returned to stoking the fire. "I understand," he said. "Duskers are dauntless hunters, you're lucky to have escaped.

They don't easily let their prey get away from them…" He looked at me expectantly, waiting for me to give him my name.

"Becca," I supplied.

Alen smiled warmly. "Nice to meet you, Becca."

I nodded, and wrapped one of his furs around me, staring at the fire between us in silence for several moments. "What's a dusker?" I asked.

"Forest lions. They often come out at dusk to hunt, which is why we call them duskers. Why, what do you call them?"

"Mountain Lions," I shrugged. "Or I guess we call them pumas, too."

"Pumas?" he chuckled. "I haven't heard that one."

"Don't they call them pumas where you live?"

"Not that I've heard," he shook his head. "Seattle must be a very different place from here. Is it a large country?"

I gave him a look, not amused. "It's a city," I said. "And I guess you could say that it's big. Traffic is pretty bad." It was rated one of the worst in the country for commutes, if I remembered exactly, but it was nowhere near New York City size. "Where are you from?" *Canada?* I wanted to add but didn't. He didn't have an accent, but there was something different about the way he spoke that felt foreign to me.

"I live here," he gestured around him. "The Timberland has always been my home."

Definitely Canada, I thought to myself with a nod. *Maybe he doesn't even know he's over the border? Or maybe he's here illegally.* Though I wasn't about to bring that up in conversation.

He caught my expression and misunderstood it. "Don't worry, Becca," he reassured. "We'll be able to reach the forest's edge in just a few days if we make good time."

I looked up in alarm at this comment, my heart beginning to race. "A few days?" I blurted. "What are you talking about? It's only a few hours hike from the campgrounds, I came out here only just today!"

"That can't be," Alen's brows knit together in an expression of suspicion. "The nearest city is four days by foot, you couldn't have gotten here in one day."

"Well I DID!" I yelled.

At that moment I was painfully aware of how still the forest was. The silence felt treacherous, like a thin layer of ice atop a vast depth of water about to crack beneath my feet.

Alen scowled and peered into the dusk, one hand rested on the hilt of a blade strapped to his belt that I had not noticed until this moment, and the sight of it did not reassure me in the slightest. "Quiet," he said softly.

"It's not wise to raise your voice in the territory of the Watcher."

I wanted to ask him what the Watcher was, but I couldn't find my voice. There was a heaviness in the air, an invisible pressure that made every hair on my body stand on end, and I knew instinctively it was the feeling of imminent danger.

Eventually he relaxed and turned to face me once more. "I don't know where you came from, or how you managed to get here. But you are here now, and if you want to survive the trip home, you'd do well to keep your voice lowered and your wits sharp. We are not alone in these woods."

I got the distinct impression he was not referring to duskers. "So, you're saying," I said, my voice much quieter, though I pronounced each word with a sharp staccato, "we are *not* in the National Park?"

He reached his stick into the fire, rolling two blackened oblong lumps out of the coals. "I don't know of any place by that name," he said gravely.

"And I suppose you've never heard of Seattle either," I scoffed.

"There are many cities I know nothing about. I've lived here all of my life, and rarely step foot out of the wood."

"And these Watchers, are you sure they aren't just Park Rangers you're trying not to get caught by?"

Alen didn't seem to know how to reply to this. He studied me for several moments, carefully rolling the objects he'd pulled from the fire into wooden bowls. "I wasn't following you," he finally said.

I didn't know what that had to do with what I asked, but I just rolled my eyes and dropped the subject. I didn't believe him, nor was I going to go along with whatever game he was playing. As long as he kept me safe from the mountain lions, I would put up with the charade, but that didn't mean I would be happy about it. *One thing's for sure*, I thought. *I never want to go camping again.*

We didn't speak to each other much after that. After a while, he handed me one of the wooden bowls with what seemed like a baked yam—one of the black things he pulled from the fire—and told me to cut it open and eat the inside. I was grateful for the food, and even though it desperately needed salt, it was warm and filling and even a little sweet. I didn't remember yams tasting quite that good. When we had finished eating, we threw the charred skins into the fire, and he gestured toward the tent with a nod. "I'll keep watch," he said.

The comment didn't encourage me, but the tent was warm, and I curled up under the furs with minimal discomfort. I thought I would stay awake like that forever, worrying endlessly about the stranger sitting just outside, the danger of mountain lions, and the invisible Watcher in the woods. But before I knew it, I had slipped quietly into a deep and dreamless sleep.

§

I was sluggish the next morning, and I did my best to help Alen roll up the furs and take down the tent. When we finished tearing down, he began to pack everything into a very weathered hiking pack that looked well past its prime.

"Ever heard of REI?" I chuckled when I saw it. He was in a serious need of some upgraded equipment if he planned on being out here camping all the time.

He looked at me curiously. "I haven't," he said. "Who is she?"

I blinked, hesitating to reply until I decided he really had no idea what I was talking about. "It's a store," I said. "You know, with camping and hiking gear? You've really never heard of it?"

"I don't really enter cities," he said, looking uncomfortable. He shouldered his pack and cleared his throat. "We should get started right away, but The Ancient Arch is not far. We can stop there to eat something if we're quiet."

"Sure," I replied indifferently. I was relieved that he wasn't making me carry anything for the walk. "What's the Ancient Arch?"

He led the way through the trees, and I followed a few paces behind him. "It was once a great doorway," he explained. "Now it is merely a broken remnant of a time long past. I never learned much of its history, but it's one of the landmarks of the forest."

I wondered if it was the same natural archway I had run through the night before, and it reassured me. It meant we were going the right way. "I don't remember it being very far, but who knows?" I murmured to myself. The fantasy game he was insisting on playing annoyed me, so I was doing my best to ignore it. As long as we made it back, I didn't care.

The walk was easy as the ground was fairly level, broken only by trees, roots, ferns and fallen branches. Occasionally the trunk of a dead evergreen would be lying in our way, and we would be forced to climb over it or go around it. On and on we walked in what seemed to me no particular direction. Everywhere I looked there was more of the same, a never-ending labyrinth of trees that seemed identical to my eyes.

It was almost an hour before we reached the edge of a small clearing, where he stopped and turned to face me with a proud smile. "Here we are," he said, stretching his hand out toward the center of the open glade. "This is the Ancient Arch. Incredible, isn't it?"

Before us stood a large stone archway, blanched white by the sun. On either side of it two trees grew up so close they were nearly a part of the stone columns themselves. They were not evergreens, in fact they looked more like maple trees by their branches, though both of them were long dead. Moss clung to their bark and to the white stones like a carpet, and intricate purple flowers dotted the lush green. I had never seen anything like it before, and yet it seemed familiar to me. Since when were there ruins in the Park like this?

I walked toward it, unnerved by the sight. "This can't be the same arch," I said, beginning to circle it to see the other side. When I reached it, I froze in place, my throat tightening in fear. It was exactly the same as the two trees I had run through last night, except for one thing. There was a path of white stone steps leading up to it that I was certain had not been there previously.

"Look," Alen remarked. I tore my eyes away from the leaning trees and saw that he was crouched on the ground on the opposite side. "Someone has been here recently. See these footsteps? They must have been in a hurry."

I walked toward him, peering down at the disturbed earth, but before I had a chance to say anything, he reached out to pick something up from the ground. He held it up curiously, turning it over in his hands with a bewildered expression, and immediately I snatched it away from him. "My phone!" I exclaimed. Why hadn't I thought to search for it before now?

Alen glanced between me and the archway, his eyes widening. "Becca," he said slowly. "Did you say you came through some trees like this when you were fleeing the dusk—the puma?" he corrected himself at the last second, and by his tone I felt like it was significant somehow.

"Yes," I said, trying to turn on my phone. It was dead and would not respond. "At least I think so. But this can't be the same one, it doesn't look right." Yet I couldn't deny that this was my phone. I felt the hairs on my neck begin to stand on end, disliking the eerie feeling growing in my stomach.

Alen stood, backing up a step. "Do you know what the Ancient Arch was supposed to do?" he asked, though it was clear by his tone he already knew my answer. He continued, hesitating only slightly. "It was a doorway. They say that it was used to travel great distances, even to other worlds."

I was afraid now. I wanted to believe that this was just a game, to be angry at him for including me in the charade without my permission, but I couldn't shake the feeling that something wasn't right. "I've had just about enough of this," I blurted. "I'm tired of the fantasy games, okay? I just want to go home."

"I don't think that's possible," Alen said, and his expression was grave.

"This door is closed, and has been for hundreds of years, perhaps even thousands."

"Stop it!" I screamed. I wouldn't believe him. I couldn't. When I spoke again, it was with much more restraint. "Stop playing games."

"Becca…" he started toward me, then halted. His face turned hard, and in a flash, he drew his blade and held it out before him, eyes fixed on something over my shoulder. The bronzed blade was deathly cold in a way that I couldn't describe, as though I could sense it more than see it with my eyes. "Get behind me," Alen ordered.

I whirled around instead. What I saw seemed unreal, and for a moment all I could do was stare. Then I laughed, though to me it almost felt like a sob that had gotten stuck in my throat. *I must be dreaming*, I reasoned.

At the edge of the clearing stood what I thought was a person on four legs, but a second look revealed a person-sized insect not unlike a praying mantis. It was green in color, with a sectioned abdomen and eyes on either side of its head, and two antennae twitching side to side as it observed us. Where a praying mantis would have two large sickle-like arms, this creature had four, and each arm sprouted three knife-like fingers, outstretched as though to grab at me. On its face was a sharp beak for a mouth, clicking as it rubbed together.

This was not something that existed in real life. This was the stuff of nightmares.

Before the insect could move, I felt Alen grab my arm and yank me backwards. I stumbled and fell to the ground, landing hard on the stone steps behind me. It hurt. "Stay back, Watcher!" he uttered sharply, stepping in front of me with his chilling sword before him.

Clicking and hissing at us, the insect skittered forward slowly, its large eyes fixed on me. It moved first to one side, then the other, letting out a sharp angry hiss as Alen followed its movements staying between it and me. Arms twitching in fury, it bent down on its digitigrade legs and sprang forward at me.

With a swipe of his blade, Alen severed two of its arms, then kicked the creature back before it could reach me. It landed several feet back, beak clicking together in a sharp snap, before it twisted around and launched at me again with incredible speed, almost like the grasshoppers I used to catch in my grandparents' backyard.

Alen was ready, planting himself between me and the bug, and ducking out of the reach of the insect's claw-like fingers. He made another swift jab with his sword, but this time it met with air as the creature avoided the strike. I couldn't keep up with their rapid movements. The cold sword slicing through the air left gusts of chill wind in its wake. A torrent of jabs and blows from the alien arms were so rapid they blended in my vision. I watched helplessly, numb at the idea that I might lose the one person who could help me get home. All I could do was sit there with my mouth open in horror.

Just as it seemed that Alen might lose, the creature leapt straight at him. At that moment, Alen twisted his hands and brought his sword upward from below with a loud yell. The blade separated the insect's head from its body, and it fell to the ground with a dying hiss, wounds seared closed by ice.

I lay upon on the stone steps with my body rigid, struggling to breathe. I could smell the creature's astringent blood, hear its flesh sizzling from the burning ice wounds, and at the back of my mind, an unsettling thought began to surface. What if this was no dream? What if…it were real?

Several seconds later I realized Alen was calling my name. I looked up, meeting his eyes, and found that I could breathe again.

"That was a Watcher," he said grimly. Even though his clothes were torn and there was blood on his face and shoulder, he reached down and offered me his hand. I took it, and his grip was firm as he pulled me to my feet. He did not let go till he was sure that I was steady. "There can be no denying now what happened."

"What *did* happen?" I asked. My voice felt distant, as my brain tried to catch up with what I had just witnessed. I couldn't believe that any of this was real, but how could I deny what I had just experienced? The doubt in my mind sent a shiver of dread down my spine.

And what do I do if it is real? Am I stuck here, forever? What if all this is just purgatory, and I'm already dead? My legs felt weak, and I nearly let myself fall down to the ground again.

Alen's face was patient as he looked at me, and he began to clean his blade, being careful not to touch it, before returning it to its sheath. "Don't you see? This doorway behind you…" he said. "You must have come through it from your world, there's no other reason they would seek you out and try to kill you."

"But what *are* they? Why would they want to kill me? It's not my fault I ended up here!" Even as the words tumbled out of my mouth defensively, I felt guilty for saying them. It *was* my fault. I went into an area I wasn't allowed to go, a place that I was warned was dangerous. In a way, I *did* deserve whatever consequences came from my stupidity, though now all I could think about was how I would never be so foolish again, if only I were just given the chance to get home. *I'll do anything, please, just don't let this be real!*

"They are the Watchers. It's said that they came from the Doorways too, once upon a time." Alen began to pace back and forth between the dead Watcher and the broken archway as he spoke, staring downward at the trodden earth. "It's said that they guard them jealously, allowing no one to pass through. This one is closed, so I had assumed they wouldn't be here. But then..." he looked at me with an incredulous expression. "You came through."

"I'm sorry," I whispered. *I want to go home. I want to see my family again.* My feelings of longing and regret were so strong, I burst into tears.

Alen came toward me, his expression awkward as he gave me an encouraging pat on the shoulder. He was quiet for a moment, watching me sob with his eyebrows furrowed in thought. "It's not going to be easy for you here, I can see that," he said quietly. "You'll need to learn how to defend yourself if you want to survive any more encounters with the Watchers."

Choking back my tears, I looked at him with unadulterated frustration. "Is that supposed to be encouraging?" I demanded. The last thing I wanted was to see another one of those things!

Almost as if I hadn't spoken, he kept going. "The nearest city is not far, at least. I don't know if you have anything of value to trade, but I am sure we could find you what you need there."

"What's the point?" I exclaimed miserably. "I don't know the first thing about this place, how am I supposed to get by when there are *monsters* out there? My phone doesn't work, I don't have any of my things, and that broken pile of rubble—" I turned and pointed accusingly at the dead archway behind me, "—was my only way home!"

Alen flinched, as though my words caused him pain. He stood in front of me in silence, his eyes not meeting my face. "That's not entirely true," he said at length.

I wiped tears and dirt from my face with my sleeve. "Right," I muttered unhappily. "There's more of these useless ruins out there, all guarded by angry nightmare bugs. Anything else I'm leaving out?"

"I could teach you," he said. His voice was so quiet I barely heard him. "If you want me to. How to fight, to travel, to hide from them."

The offer didn't exactly make me feel hopeful. "What's the point?" I asked again. "No matter what I do, it doesn't change the fact that I'm stuck here. I don't ever want to see one those things again!"

"Neither do I," Alen snapped, frustration rising in his voice. "But you're not going to make it without my protection!" He took a deep breath and added more calmly, "I'm willing...if you want me to."

I took an unsteady breath and let it out slowly. "I do want your help."

My words brought a faint smile to his lips. "I will teach you what you need to know in order to live here," he promised.

No matter how hard I tried, I could not keep my tears from spilling down my cheeks. *I don't want to live here*, I thought unhappily. *I want to go home*. But all I said was "okay."

He helped me to my feet and led the way through the trees, picking up his belongings as we passed by the body of the Watcher. I stopped to give it one last scathing glare before trodding after him. "How long did you say it would take to get to the city?" I asked hopefully.

"Only a few days," Alen replied. He looked up at the sky in thought. "Then we'll need a few days to get more provisions. The journey might take several weeks."

"What journey?" I refrained from groaning, dreading any more time spent in the wilderness. "Do we have to go tromping through the woods to avoid the Watchers? Why can't we just stay in the city?"

He turned and looked over his shoulder at me, bewildered. "Don't you want to go home?" he asked.

I just stared at him with my mouth open as I tried to figure out what to say. Of *course*, I wanted to go home! "Didn't you say the doorway is closed?" I demanded.

That same look of frustration crossed his face. "*That* doorway, yes." He glanced past me through the trees, his eyes fixed on the ruin. "But I know where to find another."

All at once, I understood his hesitation, the need for provisions, and his admonition that I would have to learn to survive.

Our eyes met and hope surged inside my chest.

There was another door.

And Alen was going to take me there.

NIWA'S MISSION

The path of the indie author is challenging and fraught with peril. The Northwest Independent Writer's Association sprang from a group of like-minded, optimistic fantasy and science fiction indies in Portland, Oregon who wanted to help each other succeed.

Almost a decade after its inception, NIWA claims over one hundred members across Washington and Oregon. Members write everything imaginable, including nonfiction, literary fiction, romance, horror, mystery, and, of course, fantasy and science fiction. Despite its diversity of membership, NIWA maintains that same indie spirit of working together to hone our craft and promote each other.

If you or someone you know is an aspiring author in the PNW, look us up at www.niwawriters.com. The group welcomes all those write, published or not. NIWA's members regularly appear across the region at conferences, conventions, and signings.

Thank you for reading this collection. If you enjoyed it, please take a moment to review it wherever you purchase books online.

Too much fantasy, sci-fi. Many typos.

Made in the USA
Middletown, DE
12 October 2020